T0129337

STUDENTS OF PAIN

From the Case Files of Max Christian, PI:

The Last Minstrel Show

The Shape-Shifters

Students of Pain

STUDENTS OF PAIN

From the Case Files of Max Christian, PI
Book 3

Peter Goldman
with
Nicola Malatesta, PI

STUDENTS OF PAIN
FROM THE CASE FILES OF MAX CHRISTIAN, PI BOOK 3

iUniverse books may be ordered through booksellers or by contacting:

iUniverse
1663 Liberty Drive
Bloomington, IN 47403
www.iuniverse.com
1-800-Authors (1-800-288-4677)

Because of the dynamic nature of the Internet, any web addresses or links contained in this book may have changed since publication and may no longer be valid. The views expressed in this work are solely those of the author and do not necessarily reflect the views of the publisher, and the publisher hereby disclaims any responsibility for them.

Any people depicted in stock imagery provided by Getty Images are models, and such images are being used for illustrative purposes only. Certain stock imagery © Getty Images.

ISBN: 978-1-5320-5227-9 (sc)
ISBN: 978-1-5320-5226-2 (e)

Library of Congress Control Number: 2018907244

Print information available on the last page.

iUniverse rev. date: 07/20/2018

For Helen, always,

and for Nicola Malatesta, PI,

my friend and partner in crime

CHAPTER 1

I Have Your Son

"So why are you here?" Max Christian asked, draining the dregs of a weak Mount Gay rum and tonic. "I thought you'd fired me."

The shade of Albert Camus had, after a long absence, settled onto the couch in the offices of Christian Enquiries; the work space occupied the garden floor of a town house bequeathed to Max, along with an $8 million trust fund, by the rich uncle who'd raised him. The late-April day outside was balmy for New York, where spring was rarely more than a comma between slushy winters and muggy summers; the sun was struggling bravely through the haze and the soot, and passersby outside had shucked their cold-weather gear for the first time in months. Camus, as always, was swathed in a heavy woolen greatcoat with the lapels turned up around his ears. His hair was slicked back, his eyebrows were arched, and his smile was knowing. The glowing stub of a Gauloise dangled from the corner of his mouth.

"I'm here 'cause you hurtin', son," he said. "I'ma be hurtin' too if you don't hook me up wid a pastis real quick."

Max poured the drink, swizzled it into a grayish-yellow cloud, and set it in front of Camus. "So I'm not fired?" he said.

"Naw, B, I jus' put your sorry ass on probation for a while

to see if you could get y'all shit together your own self. Way it look, you couldn't. Way it look, you ain't got shit else to do but feel sorry for yaself."

"You're right, Al. At least about the part where I'm hurting."

"Why I be here, bruh. Pain be real, even if it jus' in y'all head, an' it can fuck up y'all world if you let it."

"Tell me about it," Max said. His world, objectively viewed, was a mess as he approached his forty-sixth birthday, and his capacity for viewing it objectively was compromised by self-pity. His wife, Meridew, had taken refuge in her mother's manor house on the Philadelphia Main Line six years earlier; their only extended time together since then had lasted five months and had ended badly, thanks to him. His son, Jay, was a freshman at Penn and rarely available even for his promised every-other-weekend visits with his dad. Max missed his old life as a homicide detective with the NYPD and was drowning in the tedium of his new one as a PI; his boutique firm, Christian Enquiries, easily could have died of neglect if he hadn't brought in a younger, more enthusiastic partner, a black ex-cop who called himself Ahab.

He had tried hard to rebuild what was left of his self-esteem by cleaning up his act and his person. He had resumed showering and shaving every morning. He and his neighborhood barber fought, against all odds, to bring at least a semblance of governance to his unruly dark hair. He took better care that his Wrangler jeans were regularly laundered and his Lands' End blazers were freshly cleaned and pressed. He monitored his waistline and gave up beer and Blimpies to hold it in check. He kept count of his drinks and watered them with various mixers. He still slept with the temps working his reception desk, but only if they made the first move. He became a regular again at the city's asphalt basketball courts, deaf to the taunts of the younger ballers calling him the Old Dude; he had enough game left to punish them with his moves.

What his vernissage couldn't smooth over was his achy conscience. He'd read Gandhi and King and the Gospels and had mostly tried to follow their commitment to lives spent doing no harm, but he had lately discovered in himself a vocation for violence, a dybbuk he hadn't previously acknowledged was there. He didn't know where all that anger came from, and discovering its presence hurt. Even in the wreckage of his life, he'd thought better of himself than that.

"I've killed two guys in my lifetime," he told Camus. "One was trying to kill my partner; the other was trying to kill me. I can live with those, okay? I know you don't like hearing it, but those guys needed to be killed."

Camus flicked the ash from his Gauloise onto Max's prime kilim rug. "I be listenin', not judgin'," he said. "You ain't heard me beefin' about the Resistance killin' people needed killin' back in the day."

"What's eating on me, though, is my last big case. I tried to kill two guys who didn't need killing. I hated myself because of that. I still do."

"That was some invidious shit, no doubt," Camus said. "But knowin' that is halfway to fixin' it."

Max turned his palms faceup on his desk and stared at them as if they were stained with blood. "I hope you're right," he said. "It cost me my wife, my kid, and my own sense of who the fuck I am. I'll never get my life back if I don't fix it."

"You on it, B. You can't no way undo what you done."

"Almost done," Max blurted.

"Ain't no different between done and almost done, son," Camus said. "Tryin' same as doin', and you be carryin' that inside yaself long as you live. I said you was on it 'cause I know you know the bad need to stay jailed up inside. Remind you never try that shit again."

"But I did try to kill those two guys, and it's fucked up everything that matters to me."

"And you in pain behind all that. Am I right or wrong?"

"You're right."

"And pain hurt. I'm still right?"

"Right. Hurting is what pain is."

"An' the onliest way not to feel pain is not to cause it," Camus said. "You alive; you gonna hurt somebody sometime.

3

We human—that's how we do. Thing is, you don't got to do it on purpose. Feel me?"

Max shrugged. "Yeah, well, I'll try."

"Tryin' ain't enough. Flip side of them old Nike ads—jus' *don't* do it."

The intercom on Max's phone console buzzed once and then again. He picked up the receiver.

"Yo, boss," Ahab's voice said. "Your wife's on line two. She sounds kinda worried."

"Got it," Max said. He looked apologetically toward the couch, but Camus was already evanescing, a swirl of multicolored dust motes drifting through the windowpane and disappearing into space.

"Max?" Meridew said. Her voice was thick with anxiety.

"Dew. Babe, what's up?"

"I've been trying to reach Jay. Is he with you?"

"I wish, but no. Last he and I talked, it was maybe this coming weekend and maybe not. 'Depending' was how he put it. Why?"

"His coach called me, looking for him. He missed practice yesterday and today. That's not like him."

"No, it's not," Max said. Jay Christian, like his dad, was a dedicated baller—not as street-schooled maybe but an inch taller at six foot five and good enough at eighteen to have made the Penn varsity as an end-of-the-bench freshman. "You've tried his roommate? Jack Whozis?"

"Just now," Meridew said. "He hasn't seen Jay since Monday."

"And you've tried his cell?"

"Several times. I left voice and text messages, but he hasn't called back. He's usually pretty good about that." She paused. "I'm worried, Max."

"My guess?" Max said with a confidence he didn't wholly feel. "He's off somewhere with Nina, getting laid."

"You're way behind, love. Nina's history. She dropped

him—said he cared more about basketball than about her. He hasn't told you about Judith?"

"Who's Judith?"

"His new lady love. She's a junior; he's a freshman. That's a pretty big generation gap at their age, but they seem to be bridging it. They're pretty much inseparable."

"An older woman. Part of every lad's coming-of-age."

"Including yours?"

"I'm not saying. My past is past."

"Don't ask, don't tell?"

"Exactly. Have you met this Judith?"

"Yes, once, and I quite liked her. She's far more sophisticated than he is, but they seem good together. They took me to dinner on my birthday at a lovely French place in Rittenhouse Square—Le Cheri, I think it's called. After which they walked me to my car and headed off to the Westin together."

"The former Ritz-Carlton?"

"Yes, where you deflowered me when we were at Penn. I didn't have a past."

"It was consensual on your part," Max said.

"No, gleeful on my part. I was eighteen, which was pretty old to be a virgin by the late eighties—it made me feel retarded. Besides which, you were slow and gentle, and I was in love. It was quite wonderful."

"Well, if you're really worried about where Jay is, the Westin's where I'd check first," Max said. "There or the basketball court at Sixteenth and Susquehanna—that's *the* streetball venue in Philly. Either place, he'd turn his phone off—I mean, having more urgent things to do."

"You're saying I shouldn't be a panicky mom?"

"Not if you can help it. As my uncle Saul used to say—"

"'Don't borrow trouble.' I know. I'll try not to, love. I promise."

"Let me know when he turns up, babe. I'll have a daddy talk with him if you want, about answering calls from his terrified mother."

"You'll call if you hear anything?"

"Cross my heart," Max said.

"And you, love? How are you faring?"

"I think you can guess. When will I see you?"

"Soon," she said. "I don't know. A week somewhere nice while there's still some spring left? The Cape maybe? Hilton Head? Paris?"

"Where doesn't matter, Dew," he said, his tone suddenly sharp. "The question was when."

"Oh, Max, please don't be cross with me. You know I'm still just trying to sort things out. I miss us as much as you do. It's just—I don't know. New York scares me right now. After what happened."

What had happened was a Cosa Nostra hit man invading their home and holding her hostage at gunpoint till Max came back from an errand and put a bloody end to the episode. She'd fled and hadn't been home since.

"I hear you, babe. I'm sorry. Really. I seem to have a gift for saying the wrong things."

"I love you, Max," she said. "Please know that."

"Goes double for me, and you already know that," he said. "We'll do that week away when you're ready."

When they'd rung off, Max sat for a time with his elbows on his desktop and his bowed head cradled in his hands, his mind wandering a trackless, timeless waste without a GPS. It was a while—he couldn't be sure how long—before a single tap at the door fetched him back into the world. He looked up. Ahab was standing there smiling. Max waved him to the couch.

"What up, boss?" Ahab asked. "You look like your dog just died. Meridew the bearer of bad news?"

"She's just being a worrier is all. She hasn't seen or heard from our son in a couple days, and his coach hasn't seen him either."

"Prob'ly an extended booty call," Ahab said with a lascivious smile. "The rewards for being young and a baller."

"That's pretty much exactly what I told Dew. What I believe too. I was young once, y'know."

"So why you so down?"

"Apart from missing my wife? It's just that once in a while, worriers turn out to be right."

Ahab, born Marquise Parker, was a slight, tailored mocha-brown man not much more than half Max's age and nearly a head shorter. They had bonded instantly when Max tracked him down on foot patrol in a leafy sector of Queens, swinging a stick on a beat where a parking summons was a big-time bust. He'd been a promising narco undercover until he'd tried a little too hard to build a case against a Harlem preacher, politician, and drug merchant named I. M. Trubble. His efforts had earned him nothing more than his self-awarded nickname, which seemed to him to fit the futility of his pursuit; the whale he'd been hunting had turned out to have friends in city hall, One Police Plaza, and the Paolucci crime family. Ahab had no such connections, no rabbi watching his back, and no future as a cop—not, anyway, among New York's Finest.

He'd quit the force and was adrift when Max recruited him; he'd sent out résumés to every big-city department from DC to LA, but given his rep as a problem child in New York, none of them had troubled to respond. It was Max alone who had come to the rescue, seeing a lot of his own beginnings in the kid. Ahab was smart, quick, intuitive, and fearless, and he was a natural-born cop, at least a decade or so shy of being the burned-out case Max felt himself becoming.

Max had started his young apprentice on day rates, $500 plus expenses, to handle some of the drudgery of life as a PI—a runaway teen, a couple of maritals, a preppy graduating from smoking weed to skin-popping heroin. Ahab's complexion gave some of Max's society clients a bit of a start, but he got results fast, and they rewarded him with thanks, praise, and gratuities that matched or exceeded his pay. Their satisfaction had gotten back to Max, and with his own enthusiasm for the quotidian grind running low, he'd promoted Ahab to partner.

Now his protégé was stretched out on his couch with his head propped on the armrest and his eyes half closed.

"Tough night?" Max asked.

"Yeah, boss," Ahab said.

"Fuck you with that 'boss' shit. I'm nobody's boss. We're partners."

"Yeah," Ahab said, smiling, "and I'm the partner does most of the work around here, boss."

"Double fuck you," Max said, smiling back. "What'd you do last night that laid you low? Let me guess—you went up the way to Barfly or Molly Malone's and got toasted?"

"Naw, I was closing a case, and drinking on duty is off book, remember? You used to be a cop yourself—an NYPD legend, or so I heard. I just encountered a little lady trouble is all. But you of all people know how that goes, *boss*."

"Triple fuck you," Max said, still smiling, but Ahab had dozed off.

The long day waned. The sun gave up and was power-napping behind a cloud. Ahab, refreshed, had repaired to his own office, a cubicle that had once been the supplies-and-equipment room. Max sat at his desk, absently shuffling balance sheets and case files; a pallid Mount Gay and tonic reposed at his elbow, awaiting the next sip. He tried phoning and texting Jay a couple of times. That he got no answer didn't surprise him; lovemaking was better served if you put your cell in airplane mode before you got busy.

The single business call came from Leona Porterfield Paisley, an old chum of Meridew's. Her aging, ailing mother's caretaker had absconded with $13,000 in cash and, worse yet, an heirloom diamond necklace that had adorned three generations of Porterfield women. Max suggested gently that the theft was a police matter, but Leona dreaded notoriety, and discretion, she insisted, was everything in such matters. "I'll look into it myself, Leona," he promised, jotting down the details. But as soon as the call ended, he buzzed Ahab and handed off the case to him.

"I've already got a marital and a skip on my plate, boss," Ahab protested. "We think the skip's in South Beach, enjoying the hundred eighty K his partner thinks he lifted from the office safe. I should be on a flight down there right now, before the mope spends it all."

"I know you're loaded up," Max said, feeling only a small twinge of guilt, "but this one's important for the firm, and it needs young legs. You can wrap it in twenty-four hours. See if Al's available to find the skip—he's good, and he's already down that way, so it'd save us the air fare. The marital can wait."

Ahab sighed. "Right, boss," he said, and he slouched back to his cell.

Max glanced at his digital Timex, hoping for 6:00 and instead reading 4:17. Dew liked to tease him about his timepiece; he was, she said, the only man she knew who shopped for watches in a drugstore. But his serial Timexes were his fuck-you to ostentation and were as important to him as her heirloom century-old Rolex was to her. Her forebears were people of deep roots and old money; his were Jewish immigrants from Ukraine, and he himself was born a red-diaper baby, the child of folksingers in willing thrall to the CPUSA.

He was searching his memory for the words to one of their favorite union anthems, "Solidarity Forever," when the New New Girl up front buzzed him with an incoming call.

"A gentleman's on the line," she said. "He won't give his name—he just said you'll want to speak with him."

"Probably selling something," Max said. "Tell him politely to fuck off."

"He said to mention the number fifty-three to you. He said, 'Mr. Christian will understand.'"

A chill seized Max, not unlike what he'd felt when witnessing an autopsy for the first time as a newcomer to Manhattan South Homicide. He reached for a fresh glass, filled it with straight Mount Gay, and took a deep swallow.

Fifty-three was Jay's uniform number.

"I'll talk to the guy," he said. "Put him through."

"Detective Christian?" a voice said.

"Yeah. Who's calling?"

"My name is Carlo Paolucci. Perhaps you've heard of me."

9

"A.k.a. Charlie Beak, correct?"

"The penny press calls me that, Detective," Paolucci said. "My friends and business associates do not."

"And you're calling because?"

"I have your son."

The chill Max had felt turned Arctic. "You fucking what?" he said.

"I think you heard me, Detective. I have your son."

"You have him where?"

Paolucci laughed.

"If you—"

Paolucci cut him off. "If I harm him? That, Detective, will be entirely up to you. His safety, for now, is guaranteed by me. His comfort as well. He will be dining this evening on pasta alla Norma, prepared by my chef from a recipe of my aunt Agnese. For wine, I've chosen a fine Aglianico."

"He's in training," Max blurted. "He doesn't drink."

"He may want to start tonight, Detective. Again, his fate is in your hands. We should meet to discuss his situation."

"Meet when?"

"I would propose tomorrow morning at ten o'clock. Do you know Caffè Reggio on McDougal Street?"

"I've been there, yeah."

"Ten o'clock then. It's a busy public place where you'll feel safe, and in any case, I am not an assassin. Come alone."

CHAPTER 2

The Price

The meeting, Max knew, had long been destined to happen. Carlo "Charlie Beak" Paolucci had lurked in the shadows of a couple of drug-related murder cases Max had worked on, the unseen puppeteer tugging on invisible strings and banking the laundered Benjamins. His NYPD mug shot was pushpinned to the bulletin board in Max's office, and Max had had many long imagined conversations with it, always ending with the satisfying *click-click* of handcuffs and the mantra that began "You have the right to remain silent ..."

Now they were face-to-face for the first time in the flesh. The Beak was standing across a small marble-topped table from Max, his hand extended for a shake, and all Max could think of to say was "Fuck you."

His proffer rejected, the Beak lowered his hand, eased into the curlicued wrought-iron chair across from Max's, and waved for service. Two double espressos and a plate of biscotti quickly appeared; the don was plainly known to the house. The day outside was bright, but not much light made it into Caffè Reggio's interior, a murky oblong enclosed by chocolate-brown walls and dark Italianate paintings.

"I understand your displeasure, Detective," the Beak said.

"But we have business to discuss, and I hope we can discuss it in a businesslike way. As you can see, I've come alone."

"Yeah, except for that fat goombah who grabbed me and took my weapon when I got out of my car around the corner. Felt more like a full-body massage than a pat-down."

"That fat goombah, as you call him, is my chief of security," the Beak said. "His name is Gianni Giacalone, but he is more widely known—known and feared—as Il Lupo."

"The Wolf," Max said. He'd picked up some bits of Italian on a long-ago wander through Tuscany with Meridew, celebrating his early retirement from the NYPD.

"The Wolf—precisely," the Beak said. "Gianni is a child's name, or a celebrity's. Il Lupo better suits his temper and his readiness to spill blood in my defense. He will stand guard outside and will return your weapon once we have finished our business. But in this café, I am alone. You, I would suggest, are not."

"Yeah, I am," Max said.

"Except perhaps for those two *melanzane* over there?" With a toss of his head, the Beak indicated two black men sipping cappuccinos beneath a large gilt-framed painting said by the house to be *scuola di Caravaggio*.

"Don't know them," Max said without looking.

"I think you do," the Beak replied with a taut smile. "One is a former narcotics officer and now your business partner. The other is a *pentito*."

"Pentito?"

"A rat. A snitch. A traitor willing to give evidence against his benefactor to save his own skin. He calls himself Death, but he buckled at the mere threat of arrest and became your partner's prime snitch. Their presence here suggests a certain mistrust on your part, and in my world, mistrust is an impediment to doing business."

"And why would I trust a scumbag who's kidnapped my son?"

"I prefer to call your son my houseguest, and I will continue to treat him as such, unless you oblige me to do otherwise.

We have a bad history, you and I, and you are notoriously quick to anger."

"How'd you get my boy?"

The Beak smiled again. "It was surprisingly easy. He was walking across the Penn campus, when my men accosted him and invited him into their car."

"At gunpoint."

"Guns were mentioned, I believe. Displaying them proved unnecessary."

The Beak emptied a pink packet of sweetener into his espresso and stirred it with a delicacy surprising for someone in his line of work. He was the godfather of the last wholly functional Cosa Nostra family in New York, but his mug shot didn't do him justice; he reminded Max of a portrait of Lorenzo de' Medici he'd seen in Italy years before. He was a man of studied elegance—his speech was precise, his posture was correct, and his suiting was carefully tailored and subtly pinstriped in shades of blue. His frame was spare, surprisingly so for a mob boss; the Cosa Nostra was one of the last cultural enclaves in America to regard fat as a virtue. His hair was iron gray and expensively sculpted. His face was pale and fine-boned. His eyes were ice blue. His mouth was a thin razor slash between his sharp chin and the great aquiline nose that had burdened him from boyhood with his nickname: Carlo Il Becco—Charlie Beak, or, simply, The Beak.

"Your nose is epic," Max said, relishing the faint flush his words brought to the Beak's cheekbones. "It explains your nom de guerre."

"My nom de guerre, as you call it, is not, in fact, mine. As I told you yesterday, it is a creation of the tabloid newspapers, and it's gained some currency, I suppose, among my jealous rivals. My friends and employees address me as Don Carlo, as is befitting a man of honor." He gave his espresso another stir, downed what was left in a swallow, and signaled for a refill. "Can we not get on with more serious business?"

"The only business I have to discuss with you is that I want my boy back, and I want him back unharmed."

"And you shall have him back, Detective, if you do exactly as I say. Is that understood?"

"How can I say yes before I've heard your terms?"

"Must I remind you of the stakes here? I have your son."

"You say you have him," Max said. "It's show-me time."

"Tell me, Detective—would you be here if you doubted my word?"

"Fuck you. I want proof of life."

The Beak reached into his inside jacket pocket, pulled out a photo, and, with two fingers, slid it across the marble to Max. "I took this over breakfast this morning with my iPhone not two hours ago."

Max took a moment to steel himself and then looked at the snapshot. The face looking back at him was unmistakably Jay's. His sandy hair was mussed, but it usually was in the morning. His eyes said nothing. His clothing said too much: he was wearing a loose-fitting orange jumper of the color and cut favored by ISIS for the infidels it was about to behead.

Max felt a sudden stab of pain in his chest, sharp enough to make him wince. He reached for his coffee, wishing it were a drink. His hand was shaking when he picked up his cup; a splash of espresso puddled on the tabletop. He could see the Beak studying his reaction with a thin, self-congratulatory smile.

"It would seem you've come to an understanding of your son's situation," the Beak said, "and having a son of my own, I believe I can guess your feelings. Now can we talk business?"

"Talk," Max said.

"First, there is to be no police involvement of any kind, local, state, or federal. Is that clear?"

"Clear."

"Second, nothing in the media, and I include the so-called social media. Not a word, not a whisper. Also clear?"

"Clear."

"Third, I've written the fee for your son's safe return on the back of the photo. Have a look."

Max flipped the picture and saw the Beak's asking price:

$25 million. His eyes widened. "Jesus," he said. "I don't have anywhere near that kind of money."

"I'm well aware of that, Detective. I'm also aware that what assets you do have are locked up in a trust fund and are not readily accessible to you. Your late uncle—may his soul rest in peace—appears not to have considered you wholly reliable with a sizable sum of money. You were, after all, the child of Communists, or so I'm told."

"So fucking what?"

"So you have a small fortune that you can't access. But your wife is not, shall we say, similarly limited. *Forbes* has estimated her present wealth at three hundred million, with perhaps twice that much to come upon the death of her aging mother."

"You seem to know a lot about us," Max said.

"Research is a primary tool in modern business," the Beak said, "and unlike my counterparts in the other New York families, I choose, whenever possible, to act on knowledge, not impulse. What I know is that Signora Christian is a woman of great wealth. Surely she would pay a small fraction of her fortune for her son's safe return."

"But she's not here. We're separated."

"I'm aware of that too, Detective, but she is still your boy's mother—indeed, his sole parent-in-residence most of the time. I'm certain she will want to involve herself and her wealth in this matter, whether from her mother's house in the Philadelphia exurbs—Gladwyne, if I recall—or back here with you. In either case, you can hardly plead poverty. The money is there."

"It may be there," Max said, "but my wife doesn't keep twenty-five million in her checking account—most of what she's got is tied up in investments and trusts."

Again, the self-satisfied smile appeared. "I understand, Detective," the Beak said, "and I am prepared to accommodate your concerns. You and your wife will have three days' grace, starting tomorrow, to set the process in motion. After that, you will arrange to pay two and a half million dollars per day over the following ten business days."

"You're joking, right?"

"I flatter myself that I am but one attribute short of being a true Renaissance man, and that is a sense of humor where business is concerned. I am deadly serious, Mr. Christian, and I advise you to be serious as well. Do we understand each other?"

"I understand what you're saying," Max said, "but moving that kind of money is a complicated process. There are all kinds of rules and regulations."

"I'm aware of that, Detective, having had occasion to transfer even larger sums myself. But I'm sure your wife's bankers will find ways to accommodate so valued a client. It will be best for all concerned if they do."

"Meaning?"

"Meaning that the late fee for missed payments will be an additional two and a half million per business day."

"Ten percent a day?" Max growled. "That's shylock math. A dressed-up knockdown loan."

"I suppose there is a distant family resemblance," the Beak said. "But in what you call shylock math, there is no penalty to the debtor who makes his payments in full and on time. Understood?"

"Understood."

"The payments are to be transferred by wire from your wife's bank or banks to my corporate account, Agnese Worldwide Enterprises, in Vanuatu."

"Vanuatu? Where's that?"

"In the South Pacific. A chain of lovely islands, or so I'm told—I've never been there. Their generous banking laws have not required my physical presence even for a day."

"You bailed on Guatemala? You had a nice little tax shelter going there—what the feds say anyway."

"I maintain a reduced presence there, but given the interest of the feds, as you call them, my legal and financial teams thought it best that I blur the lines a bit. I move money through accounts in several business-friendly countries now, and Vanuatu seemed best for this transaction." He dipped back into his inside pocket and handed Max a sealed envelope.

"You'll find the required banking information here. Again, are my terms understood?"

Max propped his elbows on the table and rested his chin on his intermeshed fingers. For a moment, he stared at Jay's frozen likeness in the photo. When he spoke, his voice was low. "We'll do it."

"A wise choice," the Beak replied. "But I have one more demand to make of you. You must accept that the money I've asked is owed me."

"Fucking owed you?"

"Just as I said. Think of the payments as reparations."

"*Ransom* is a more accurate word. How do I owe you reparations?"

"How do you not owe me? You and your associates have cost me two important earners and two of my most valued soldiers, all now in the ground. Some of your *mulignana* friends—"

"Mulignana?"

"Moolies. Eggplants. Niggers. Some of your mulignana friends murdered my older brother, Giuliano. My brother, Detective. Blood of my blood."

Paolucci paused for a long moment, contemplating his neatly manicured fingernails. When he resumed, the anger in his voice had given way to fatalism, and his icy eyes glittered. "I am," he said, "an understanding man, and I'm willing to write off those losses as the fortunes of war. They were all coarse, violent men, and yes, I include my brother in that number. I loved him, and he served me as my underboss. But he was a throwback, an anachronism, a nineteenth-century Sicilian *brigante* unable to adapt to a twenty-first-century corporate world. For him, accounts could be settled only in blood."

"Which made him expendable? Your own brother?"

The Beak gave a short, quick turn of the wrist, as if flicking the ash off a cigarette. "He had become a dead weight on the Paolucci *borgata*," he said.

"Borgata? I thought that was a casino hotel in Atlantic City."

"Please don't try my patience, Detective. In your years as a police officer, it surely could not have escaped you that in this thing of ours, *borgata* is an alternate term for family. It's unbecoming of you to feign ignorance."

"My apologies, *Don Carlo*, but let me get this straight. You've just forgiven me my sins, and I still owe you twenty-five million if I want my son back?"

For a long moment, the Beak gazed out a vertical slit of window beside him, out at the flow of shoppers and tourists through the polyglot remains of what once had been Little Italy. "It is," he said, turning back to Max, "a matter of necessity, not revenge. You are aware, I'm sure, of the trumped-up racketeering charges pending against me, and twenty-five million is my best estimate of what it will cost to defend myself."

"But why am I paying your legal bills? That's a RICO case. RICO's a federal statute. I had nothing to do with your problems."

"Not directly, no. But your present partner made a highly compromising video of my most prolific business associate in upper Manhattan."

"That would be the Reverend Trubble," Max said. "The hump who moved your shit in Harlem and got caught on camera doing it."

"Caught by your partner in his days as an undercover narcotics officer."

"So just out of curiosity, why isn't he responsible for your legal bills? Why me?"

"He is not independently wealthy," the Beak said, "and he doesn't have a son."

"And his video will kill you in a RICO case. If Trubble coughed and you said, 'Bless you'—bang!—you're party to a criminal conspiracy, looking at twenty-five in supermax."

"That, Detective," the Beak said, "is what your federal colleagues hope will be the outcome. In fact, I was merely an investor in a group of clubs and lounges operated by Mr. Trubble, mostly in Harlem. The yield on my investment was quite lucrative. What the reverend did or sold in his clubs was of no concern to me so long as the dividends kept flowing. I never visited any of his establishments; I never asked the secret of his success. My single concern, as an investor, was the net-net. The bottom line."

Max laughed a sharp one-ha laugh. "So you're the poor, innocent bystander," he said, "and yet you're twenty-five million worth of worried? Ginzo, please. Your investment was lucrative because you were running drugs through those clubs with Trubble fronting for you."

Ice crystals danced in the silence between the two men. "Don't provoke me, Detective," the Beak said, his voice at whisper level. "Not while your son is my guest."

"Like I forgot, right?"

"I'm twenty-five million worth of worried, to borrow your unfortunate phrase, because Mr. Trubble has chosen to turn on the man who made him rich. He is—or was—my codefendant in the government's manufactured conspiracy case, but he has turned on me to save himself. Your partner's video made his position unsustainable. Rather than face the consequences, he has chosen a more agreeable form of incarceration—"

"WitPro? Witness protection?"

"In return for bearing witness against me. He is my Judas."

"I thought snitching only occurred in other families. I thought you'd rat-proofed yours."

"So I had, perhaps foolishly, come to believe. There were a few turncoats early in my tenure as *padrino,* succeeding my father. I made examples of them and have had no problems since."

"How'd you manage that?"

"I introduced them to days and levels of pain so severe that they begged for death. When I had Il Lupo oblige them, it was not so much murder as mercy killing."

"I see why you've been called a student of pain," Max said.

"A student," the Beak said, "and a connoisseur. As the Marquis de Sade tells us, it is by way of pain that one arrives at pleasure. For him, of course, the pleasure was sexual. For me, pain is strategic and, even more, aesthetic. I regard it as an art form."

"If you practice that art form on my son, you're a dead man."

19

There was no warmth in the Beak's answering smile. "I won't bother asking how you think you could manage that," he said. "I will simply repeat my guarantee to you: no harm will come to your son so long as he behaves himself and you keep the terms of our business agreement. He will experience at most a peek at what awaits him if you default on your payments."

"A peek?"

"A peek to assure his full awareness of his situation. You are familiar with the plays of Bertolt Brecht?"

"Some of them, yeah."

"*Galileo?*"

"It's been since college, but yeah, I've read it. Why?"

"You may recall that Galileo stands accused of heresy, but the newly anointed pope directs that he is not to be tortured. He is, after all, a man of science. Just show him the implements, His Holiness decrees. He will understand."

"You son of a bitch," Max said.

The Beak rose to leave. "Your first payment is due Friday, three days from tomorrow," he said. "Your son's future is in your hands."

"I want to talk to him. I need to be sure you haven't hurt him."

"That can be arranged. I will allow you five minutes with the boy on Skype tomorrow morning. At ten again, shall we say?"

Max nodded. The Beak once again extended his hand. Again, Max ignored it. The Beak shrugged and headed out onto McDougal Street, where a vintage black Lincoln Continental awaited him with its engine running.

Max stepped outside to collect his SIG from Il Lupo and watched the Lincoln melt into the eastbound glut of traffic on Houston Street.

"Fuck you, Beak," the red-eyed savage caged inside him said. "You're fucking dead."

Matt Mullarkey was sipping a Brooklyn Lager in the Minetta Tavern, just down the block, when Max slid onto the stool beside him. Mullarkey was a retired NYPD detective who looked more like a barkeep in Hell's Kitchen before the gentrifiers moved in. In fact, his white thatch, ruddy face, and tenor pipes were items of disguise. The Real Mullarkey had made himself a master of the black arts of surveillance; in his years on the job, it was said that old Matty could tap any phone in the city from a basement box three or four blocks away.

He was a specialist among the generalists on Max's bench, the roster of off-duty and retired detectives he called on for spot assignments and generously rewarded. Mullarkey in turn respected Max's squeamishness about electronic surveillance; he submitted his findings in written reports and attributed their content to "a confidential informant," allowing Max at least the pretext that the source was nonelectronic.

"So'd you get all that?" Max asked.

"Got it all, boyo," Mullarkey said. "Had my Dixie cup to the wall the whole time."

He'd met Max at a corner deli before the Reggio summit and handed him a pair of glasses. "Wear these," he'd said.

"Why?" Max had asked.

"If I tell you, lad, it'd be one of those things gives you a case of the collywobbles. Just wear them. They're naught but window glass."

"But I don't wear glasses."

"Does Mr. Beak know that, boyo?"

"Probably not, no."

"His boys will pat you down before you go in to see if you're wearing a wire," Mullarkey had said. "But they won't look at your glasses. They never do."

"You know how I feel about this stuff."

"You have to learn to share, boyo. You wouldn't have me parked across the street with nothing to do but whistle 'Danny Boy' and pound my withered pud, would you?"

"Not a pretty picture," Max had said; he'd surrendered and worn the glasses, and neither the Beak nor his muscle had given them a second glance. Now, in the muted light of the Minetta Tavern, he let himself be pleased that a stunt he'd resisted knowing about had actually come off.

"Although I'm not sure why you wanted it, boyo," Mullarkey said. "The man told you not to tell the police or anybody else about your lad."

"But if I get him back"—superstition wouldn't allow Max to say *when*—"I'll drop a kidnapping charge on top of the shit pile he's already looking at."

"Understood," Mullarkey said. "You'll have my CI's account tonight. I buy you one in the meantime?"

"I'm buying," Max said, waving at the bartender. He ordered another beer for Mullarkey and a double Jack for himself, with a Bud back.

"Whoa, boyo," Mullarkey said with more concern than reproof in his tone. "It's still morning. I thought you were easing up on the spirits a wee bit."

"Not today," Max said. "I've gotta call Meridew, and I'm dreading it."

"You haven't told her?"

"I haven't fucking told her. Say it, Matt—I'm a coward and a pussy. I know that's what you're thinking."

"No, lad," Mullarkey said. "What I'm thinking is you're human."

Max gulped half his Jack D, chased it with a swallow of beer, finished the Jack, and gestured for another. Mullarkey said nothing.

"I swear to God," Max muttered, "I'm gonna kill that motherfucker."

"Easy there, boyo," Mullarkey said. "I shouldn't have to remind you the both of us are still sworn to uphold the law."

"Fuck the law," Max said, his voice a feral growl. "This is a street beef. He's dead."

It was only then that he noticed Camus's ghost watching him, sad-eyed, from a stool at the far corner of the bar. They stared at one another for a silent moment; then Camus shook his head, averted his eyes, and dematerialized, leaving behind a half-finished calvados and the smoldering stub of a Gauloise.

CHAPTER 3

The Prisoner

Afterward, he would wonder why he had so dreaded making the call, and he could only conclude that he had once again underestimated his wife. He had expected a storm of emotions—of tears for their son and anger at her husband for having drawn his family yet again into the darkness he had chosen for himself. He had forgotten how good she was—how good women could be—in crises. He had drowned his own fear in bloodlust and Mount Gay Eclipse rum. She had channeled hers into purpose.

"I swear it, Dew," he'd said. "I'll kill that guido motherfucker. I will."

"And get Jay killed in revenge?" she'd replied. "*Lex talionis*? An eye for an eye? No, think, Max. You're not thinking."

"I'll get Jay back somehow—I swear it. I'll figure out some kind of way. But I want that motherfucker's ass."

"No, Max. We've got to do what he says. It's the only way we'll ever see our son again."

"By buying him back from this bloodsucker?" he'd said. "Dew, *you're* not thinking. Paolucci told me himself he's a student of pain—he fucking told me that. Told me he gets an aesthetic kick out of torturing people for days until they beg to die. A sadist like that—what guarantee do we have that he'd keep his word even if we pay?"

"There'll be no guarantees whatever we do," she'd said. "But if we don't pay, we're guaranteeing we'll never see Jay again—can we at least agree on that?"

Max had poured himself a drink and then sat for a silent moment, wondering why he'd poured it. The glass had stood untouched on his desk, a monument to his fading fantasies of revenge. His years as a cop had taught him the math: kidnap victims were rarely returned alive, even if you paid the ransom. And if you didn't? If you tried to free them by force? They all died.

"You're right, babe," he'd said finally. "As always. We don't have a choice."

"No," she'd said. "We don't."

"But how do we get it done? That's a lot of money for a bank to be moving without the feds asking questions we can't answer."

"I'm guessing Edith can make it happen. It's pretty much her bank now, and she's been my best friend since nursery school."

Edith was Edith Clift, a principal in the venerable Philadelphia banking firm of Clift, Clift, Cumming, Fleming, and Smith. She had come into her large holdings by inheritance on the untimely death of her husband, Henry Worthington Clift IV, the billionaire scion of the bank's reigning family; his throat had been slit by the last in a long train of cast-off girlfriends he'd seduced with promises of fame, fortune, and everlasting love. Edith's interest in the day-to-day operations of the family business was slight beyond its management of her own nine-figure fortune. With Henry gone, she'd sold off his Beaux Arts mansion in Manhattan, her prison for the twenty years of their marriage, and was living in Paris with a new beau—a writer who actually loved her.

"Can she make it happen?" Max had asked. "I mean, she's three thousand miles away, and we've gotta get this moving. I mean, we've only got seventy-two hours."

"There are telephones," Meridew had said. "I'm pretty sure

that if Edith calls, somebody senior will answer. She's a part owner, and I'm their biggest single client."

"But can the two of you get it done without telling anyone why you need to move twenty-five million? To fucking Vanuatu? In ten business days?"

"We'll see, won't we?"

"I'll email you the banking information right now. You'll get on it?"

"I'll call Edith as soon as we hang up."

"And you'll be here—when?"

"Sometime this evening, love. I'll call you from the train. I want to be there for Jay in the morning."

"If that fucker Charlie Beak keeps his promise. I want to—" He'd interrupted himself and taken a longing look at the drink sitting untouched at his elbow.

"Max?" she'd said. "Don't go back there."

"Back where?"

"That place. That anger. It's not good for Jay. For any of us."

He'd sighed. "How are you so damn level-headed?"

"I'm not," she'd said, her voice thickening. "I'm scared, love."

It had come to him only then that she'd been fighting back tears the whole time. He'd reached for his glass and taken a deep swallow.

"So am I, babe," he'd said. "So am I."

They embraced and kissed in the dour light of Penn Station when Meridew arrived at nightfall. She was carrying only a black Tumi weekender, which felt alarmingly light to Max when he picked it up.

"It's okay, love," she said, doubtless seeing the disappointment in his eyes. "I expect to be doing some commuting until we're sure the money's flowing on time."

"You spoke with Edith?" Max asked.

"Mm."

"And?"

"First words out of her mouth when I told her the situation? 'No problem.' You know Edith."

"And then?"

"I gave her all those banking numbers and codes— whatever. She took them all down and told me not to worry; she'd take care of it. An hour later—actually, less than an hour—she got back to me. She'd spoken to Henry's father, and he said he'd take care of it. I'd just have to show up and sign papers as needed."

"He's pretty old. I thought he'd retired."

"As managing partner, yes. But he's still board chairman; he still comes to work every day. Trust me—if he says, 'Frog,' everybody in the building still jumps."

"And he'd do this for us?"

"He'd do it for Edith. He always loved her more than his own son, and it wasn't she who scandalized the family name. You'll recall he didn't even come to Henry's funeral. Henry hurt them both. They were collateral damage."

"Bless the old man," Max said. "Bless Edith."

Max swung left into Eighteenth Street, into traffic backed up by the construction projects devouring the city. Horns honked. A car alarm yowled. An aged beggar hovered at Max's car window; Max dug into his Wranglers, found a crumpled twenty, and handed it over. "God bless you," the old man said, shuffling off. The van ahead of Max crept forward by about a car length and then stopped. Max stayed in place to let a couple of jaywalkers cross. "Move it, fuckhead!" the driver behind him yelled, as if a car length represented progress. Max shrugged and turned to Meridew.

"I hate what this is costing you," he said.

She met his gaze, a tinge of anger in her eyes. "The money doesn't matter," she said.

"I didn't mean the money. You're his mother."

"And you're his father. This is costing *us*."

"That's what I was trying to say—I just said it badly. I fathered Jay, yes—I was the sperm donor. You bore him and raised him, mostly alone, while I was out chasing bad guys. The cost is inherently higher for the mother—that's all I meant. Honest, babe."

Meridew reached out and took his hand. "Oh, Max," she said.

He glanced at her. The flash fire in her eyes had yielded to the glimmer of tears.

"It's going to be okay, babe," he said. "I promise."

It was nearly nine when they got clear of traffic and made it home. Max poured drinks while Meridew scrambled a half dozen eggs; neither of them had the stomach for anything more challenging. They ate in silence and cleared the table. The dishwasher was still clanking in the background when they retired to their bedroom and made love hungrily but slowly, seeking a oneness they both would need to be strong for Jay in the morning.

"Don't be angry with me, Dew," Max said afterward, lying awake in the darkness.

Meridew rolled close and laid a hand on his chest. "How could I be angry with you, love?" she said. "None of this is your fault."

"In a way, it is."

"Oh please, Max. The man is a criminal, he's somehow decided that we should pay for his lawyers, and he knows that we have what he needs—end of story. If it's anybody's fault, it's mine for being stupid rich. I made us a target."

"No, babe, I'm the target. Mr. Beak's got way more than he needs for his lawyers—the guy controls more of the drug traffic in New York than the other four mob families combined. This is a grudge thing for him, a Sicilian thing. He blames me for a lot of stuff, and he's not all wrong."

"What stuff?"

"Just stuff. You don't need war stories from me, not right now. I just feel like I brought this down on our heads."

"Oh stop, love. Let's either try to sleep, or we could—"

"Yeah, we could, babe," he said, taking her in his arms again.

"Good morning, signore *e* signora," the Beak, or his distorted likeness, said when the Skype chat began at precisely ten o'clock. The medium was kind only to the homely, and Don Carlo Paolucci was not that. In life, he looked like a quattrocento Florentine prince misplaced in time. On Skype, he more nearly resembled a man drowning in an aquarium.

"Skip the bullshit," Max said. "We're here to see our son. Where is he?"

"Rest assured you will see him, and you will see that he is unharmed," the face in the fish tank replied. "But first, I would like a progress report on our, ah, business transaction. Signora?"

Meridew had been near tears all morning, but when she responded, her voice was steady, and her manner was cool. "As you're no doubt aware," she said, "there is a great deal of paperwork involved in moving large sums on short notice. But my bankers assure me that it can be done. On your timetable."

"And you didn't tell them why you might want to wire such sums to an obscure corporate entity in Vanuatu? In so great a hurry?"

"Let's say I have some leverage with them, given the amount of money I've entrusted to their care. And they're old-school Philadelphia bankers. They're far too discreet to ask questions. They cater to Society with a capital *S*."

"A caste to which you belong?"

"By birth, not by disposition," Meridew said. She smiled and squeezed Max's hand. "Nor by marriage, certainly. I thought appearing at teas and salons with a policeman on my arm would be my ticket out. No such luck—marrying Max got me marked down as an eccentric, but absent scandal, Society is a life sentence."

"But these bankers you so trust," the Beak said. "Would

they not alert the authorities to, let's say, unusual transactions of a certain scale?"

"And offend a top-shelf client they might see at the country club the following weekend? I don't think so. Of course, your experience with banks has doubtless been different from mine."

The Beak smiled. "Indeed," he said. "It's why I prefer banking in countries where discretion is a matter of law, not social standing. So I may expect a first installment by Friday?"

"Yeah, fuckhead," Max said. "Can we see our son now?"

"You may, Detective. In the society *I* was born into, we refer to one another as men of honor, and a man of honor keeps his word. You may have five minutes to chat with your boy."

"Five minutes? What the fuck?"

"Five minutes should be quite enough time for you to convey your best wishes and reassure yourselves that he is unharmed. Anything longer would allow your man Mullarkey more time to try to trace this conversation. My IT director assures me it can't be done, but I like to err on the side of caution."

Max spent a numb moment wondering how the fuck the Beak knew about Mullarkey, what else he shouldn't know but maybe did, and what a mob boss was doing with an IT director in the first place. He was still puzzling when he heard the Beak say, "Jay, you're on. Behave."

Jay materialized in the murk onscreen, still wearing the ISIS-orange jumper. He was attempting a poker face, but his eyes, for those who knew him, were tells: they said he was scared.

"Mom, Dad," he said.

"Jay," Meridew said, her voice thick with fear, "are you all right? Has this man hurt you in any way?"

"No, Mom—not yet."

"Jay," a voice offscreen said sharply.

"I mean, what I meant to say is, they've, like, treated me okay so far. I mean, I've got my own room—I mean, there's someone in it with me all the time, but it's got a plasma TV and Xbox, and I've got my textbooks from when they, uh, when they picked me up, so I can sort of keep up with my schoolwork. I'm just scared—" He glanced at something or someone offscreen and then turned back to the camera.

"Scared about what, Son?" Max asked.

"I'm, like, scared Coach will go batshit 'cause I've been missing practice. He could red-shirt me for next season or maybe totally kick me off the team."

"Like father like son," Max said, forcing a smile. He'd been booted from Penn's freshman squad in his day for bringing too much ghetto-fabulous styling to his game. "Don't worry, Jaybird," he said, straining to sound reassuring. "I'll talk to Coach and make up something about how I'm in the ICU with tularemia and you're home helping Mom take care of me—something sad like that. I'll talk to the dean too—they'll understand."

"You're not real cool at making shit up, Dad."

"Won't matter. We'll have you out of there before they figure out I'm lying. You okay meanwhile? You look kinda worried. Did, ah, Mr. Paolucci do something or maybe show you something that scared you?"

Again, Jay glanced quickly off camera, and when he answered, the words sounded prescreened. "Well," he said, "he walked me through this sort of private museum of torture gizmos going back to the Middle Ages and before. He says it's the best private collection on the planet—way better than most of the ones in torture museums over in Europe. He told me what each one does, how bad it hurts, and how much you can stand till you're either, like, dead or wish you were dead."

"Did he threaten you with any of it?"

"No, not like that. He told me I'd be his guest for a little while, and he'd treat me like a guest as long as I behave— that's a word he uses a lot."

"Behave how?"

"Mostly, it's all good if I stay in my room and study or watch TV. I eat with him and that fat guy who's always around."

"The one he calls Il Lupo? The Wolf?"

"Yeah, that's him. He never says much, just kinda eats and grunts. Mr. Paolucci does most of the talking."

"What about?"

"A lot about his son, Luca—how he got an MBA at Stanford and is helping his dad some with business decisions. Says we'd like each other. He hopes we'll get to meet while I'm here."

"Here?" Max said, knowing he was on dangerous ground. "Where's here?"

Jay glanced off camera again.

"Behave," a voice said in a stage whisper loud enough to be heard.

When Jay turned back to the camera, his voice was choked, and the angst in his eyes had escalated to something nearer terror. "I don't know," he said.

"You don't know," Max said, "or you're scared to say?"

"I don't know. For real, Dad. I had, like, a hood over my head the whole time I was in the car. All I know is, it was a long ride getting here."

"What is it? City? Country?"

"I don't even know that. My room is all, like, soundproofed, and it doesn't have any windows. Only way I even know if it's day or night is mealtimes and watching TV."

"And where you eat meals? Doesn't it have windows?"

"Yeah, but it's like they keep the drapes pulled tight all the time. Like they don't care about seeing out as long as no one outside can see in."

Again came the whisper from the wings, louder and sharper this time: "Behave!"

"They're creeping me out in here. For real. You've gotta get me out of here, Dad."

"Jaybird, your mom and I are working on it, and we will get you home as soon as we can. Mr. Paolucci has set a price, and we're meeting it, but we need you to be strong for us until we're paid up. You think you can hang tough a little longer?"

"How much longer?"

"A couple of weeks max. Sooner if we can."

"A couple of weeks?" Jay's eyes suddenly flooded. "I'll never make it. No fucking way. I need to be outa here like yesterday. Dad? Mom? Please—I'm scared. He'll put me back in the—"

"Enough!" the voice from the wings said. "He's misbehaving. Take him to his room, and tell him I'll be seeing him later."

When one of Jay's jailers yanked him to his feet, Max and Meridew could see for the first time that his wrists and ankles were manacled. Meridew turned away and left the room, taking her tears off camera. Max could hear her footsteps on the stairs up to their living quarters.

"What was he trying to tell us?" he demanded when the Beak reappeared on the screen. "You'll put him back in what?"

"I keep a special place for naughty children," the Beak said, his tone gelid. "It's called a little-ease. Your son occupied it once for fifteen minutes for acting up, and it seemed to have a salutary effect on his behavior, at least till now. We'll try thirty minutes this time."

"What the fuck is a little-ease?"

"Look it up. It will deepen your understanding of the delicacy of your son's situation. For now, this session is over."

"Just a fucking minute. If you so much as—"

"I understand you're upset, Detective—I'm a father too. But threats are idle if they cannot be carried out."

"But we've agreed to pay you what you've asked," Max said. "The first transfer should reach your account by your deadline—probably before your deadline. Shouldn't that buy a little leniency for my son?"

"My leniency depends solely on your behavior and his while he is my guest. For now, I would propose that we resume this dialogue face-to-face, man-to-man. Skype is such an imperfect medium, and I'm afraid today's chat was a bit hard on your wife."

"Where and when?" Max asked.

"I'll call you," the Beak replied.

CHAPTER 4

Just This Side of Nowhere

"So what's a little-ease?" Max asked, poking his head into Ahab's cubicle. "You Google it?"

"You sure you want to know, boss?" Ahab said. "You ain't gonna like it."

"I need to know—want's got nothing to do with it. We're talking about my son."

"Okay, boss, but it ain't pretty. A little-ease is like a small cage—I mean real small. When you're in there, you can't stand up, lie down, or even sit without bending yourself all up like a pretzel. The Brits supposedly had one in the Tower of London back in the 1500s, but evidently, they were all over Europe those days. If the king's boys thought you did something, said something, or thought something, or maybe they just didn't like your ass, they put you in that box long as it took to get your mind right. You're in there long enough, you never walk right again."

"You said small. How small?"

Ahab took a few seconds before answering. "In olden times? Four by four by four. Maybe the Beak's is a little bigger—I mean, everybody being taller now."

"Four by four by four?" Max said. "Fuck me. Jay's six five."

"Told ya you wouldn't like it, boss. We're lookin' at a class A psycho here."

Max planted his fingertips on Ahab's desk and lowered himself unsteadily into the one guest chair.

"You okay, man?" Ahab asked. "You don't look so good—all pale and shit."

"I don't feel so good."

"Get you a drink?"

"Yeah, that'd work."

Ahab headed for Max's office and reappeared with a strong pour of Mount Gay. Max took an experimental first sip, decided he'd survive it, and allowed himself a less tentative swallow.

"Join me?" he said.

"Never on duty, boss," Ahab answered, smiling. "The book is the book."

"I have to remind you you're not a cop anymore?"

"Seems like I kinda am. Seems like you, me, and Mullarkey just became a major-case detail."

"Mullarkey find out anything useful?"

"Not much. He wired himself into the Skype call—don't ask me how—and tried to track it from his place. Said your idea of surveillance equipment is pre-Copernican, whatever that means."

"You should see his apartment," Max said. "It's a one-bedroom in Astoria with no bed in the bedroom—that's where he keeps his electronic toys. He sleeps on a fold-out couch in the living room."

"No wife? He's wearing a ring."

"Marie died maybe fifteen years ago. No wife, no job, so he turns their bed chamber into a mini-NSA. Fuck, the NSA would probably be jealous if they saw the stuff he's got in there."

"What's he live on?"

"Cheese crackers with peanut butter mostly—that and Brooklyn Lager. He said his appetite died when Marie died."

"No, I meant what does he do for money? I mean, that electronic shit ain't cheap."

"He does okay. He retired as a detective first grade, so

his pension's gotta be at least sixty or seventy K, plus Social Security, plus whatever gigs he gets from us and a couple of other PIs who require his skill set." Max downed another healthier swallow of rum. "But you're saying he couldn't track the call?"

"He hasn't given up, but he said it's gonna be tougher than he expected. He thinks your friend Don Carlo maybe has a private server—you know, like what Hillary Clinton used for her email and shit? Or a VPN."

"What's a VPN?"

"Fuck if I know, boss—all I could think of was vodkas per night. If you're pre-Copernican, which I'm guessing means retarded, I'm pre-you."

"So we're nowhere?"

"Just this side of nowhere. Mullarkey says we can pretty much rule out Lido Beach—you know, where Beaky supposedly lays his head? Or anywhere else on the island, for that matter. He said, 'Tell Max from what we know so far, the compass points north, not east.' Said it could be uptown, could be the Bronx, and could even be Westchester County. Or maybe farther—like maybe he's got a spread upstate. That's how some dons do."

"That's fucked up," Max said. "Doesn't fit anything we know about the Beak. What makes Matty think any of that?"

"Please, boss," Ahab said. "You trust him?"

"On tech stuff? With my life, and right now? My son's."

"So let him work, okay?"

"Okay, yeah, you're right," Max said. He sighed, picked up his drink, and rose carefully to his feet, testing his shaken equilibrium. "But when he calls back, see if we can get him to come in and sweep our offices. Upstairs too."

"C'mon, boss," Ahab said. "You ever known a mob guy who planted a tap or a bug?"

Max snorted. "You ever known a mob guy like Charlie Beak?" he said. "Talked like Charlie Beak? Dressed like Charlie Beak? Got an IT guy like Charlie Beak? He's not like any I've seen—that's for sure. The guy's smart, he's fastidious, and he thinks two or three moves ahead, which is how he's survived in the age of RICO. Big Paulie's dead, Chin's dead, and Vinny Gorgeous is doing life in supermax. The Beak has outlasted them all."

"Until now," Ahab said.

"Until now, but I wouldn't bet against him skating this time. It's not dumb luck keeps him going. How you think he knew Mullarkey was trying to track his calls?"

"Unless he was hearing what we're saying up in here," Ahab said, sounding sheepish. "You're right—I'll get Mullarkey on it, 'less you want to talk to him."

"Can't right now. You call him. On your cell."

"You headed out, boss?"

"Yeah, in a few minutes," Max said, hovering in the doorway. "Gotta get with Meridew first, though, partner."

Dew was halfway downstairs when Max started up. Her tears had dried, but the fear lingered in her amber eyes. Max took her hand, and they sat down together on a middle step.

"What is that … that …"

"That motherfucker?" he prompted. "That the word you're groping for?"

"What is he doing to Jay?"

"Ahab looked up *little-ease* while we were still on the call. It's just a small cell, like solitary in prison. A little like a kid being sent to the corner for acting up in class. He'll be okay."

"Don't lie to make me feel better, Max. I Googled *little-ease* too. I know what it is, and it's nothing like sitting in the corner. It's a box, Max. A small box. It's torture."

Max slid an arm around her shoulders and tugged her close. "He's a tough kid," he said, trying to sound assured. "Tougher than you think. It's a half hour. He'll be okay."

A single tear started down Meridew's cheekbone. Max wiped it away gently with a thumb.

"I know what I'm gonna do," he said.

"What are you thinking?"

"I'm gonna spring him."

"How, love? How?"

He wished he knew. "Trust me, babe," he said. "I'm on it."

Max headed back to his office, knowing what his first move would be. En route, he looked in on Ahab again, pressed a finger to his lips, and gestured toward a boom box on the desk. It was Ahab's comfort food for the soul, a reminder of his roots in the Brooklyn projects. When he and Max were both in residence, he stuck to low-decibel old school, a taste the two men shared, but reading Max's meaning, he clicked to a hip-hop station, kicked up the volume, and caught a Dr. Dre track from *Straight Outta Compton.*

Sheltered by the sound, Max waved Ahab out into the hallway and asked if he'd arranged the sweep.

"Mullarkey says we'll do better if he sticks to job one, tracking that call," Ahab said. "Said he'd send his kid brother, Jamie, to do the bug hunt."

"Never knew he had a kid brother," Max said. "The kid could be sixty or sixty-five, 'cause Matt's not exactly a spring chicken. This Jamie know what he's doing?"

"Mullarkey says Jamie knows more about electronic surveillance than he does. Says he learned most of what he knows from the kid. Says Jamie's also an el primo hacker, which Mullarkey isn't."

"So maybe Jamie should be doing the tracking?"

"He's been up at Mullarkey's, working on it all day. We're gonna need to cut him a separate check."

"Approved," Max said. "Do it, get him here, and stay off the landlines till he's done, okay?"

"Okay."

"And now turn that thing off soon as this track's done, so we can play to our invisible audience."

"Cool, boss," Ahab said. "Live from Eighteenth Street, Christian Enquiries presents the aged Willie Nelson and the ageless Ray Charles, together in concert!"

"Fuck you," Max said. "Get serious. Remember the stakes."

"Sorry, boss. My bad."

"Forget it. Here's the deal—they know I'm worried about a bug. They heard me say I want a sweep. So you come in my office and tell me it isn't happening, and I ask how come, and you say—I don't know. Wing it. Make shit up."

"Got it," Ahab said. He ducked back into his cubbyhole, shut down the music, and headed back to Max's office, humming "Seven Spanish Angels" to himself.

And action, Max mouthed.

Ahab nodded.

"Anything new from Mullarkey?" Max asked aloud.

"Naw, boss, no luck tracking the call. He's close to giving up."

"You told him we needed a bug exterminator?"

"Yeah, I told him."

"And?"

"He said, 'Tell Max he's fucking crazy'—his words, not mine. Said, 'There's a reason these Mafia goombahs don't do taps and bugs, boyo. They're too fucking dumb.' Said he gets that you're scared for your son, but scared is one thing; paranoia's another."

"He's saying he won't do it?"

"He didn't quite say *won't*, but that was pretty much the message. Said, 'Tell Max to get back on his meds and save the money.' And you know what, boss? He's right."

Max let most of a minute slip by in silence. "Yeah," he said finally, "he's right. I've let the fucker get to me. Only bug he's probably planted is inside my skull."

Another half minute slid away.

"He's the student of pain, and I'm his fucking lab rat. If I let him drive me nuts, he wins."

There was silence.

"I gotta get out of this little-ease he's got me in—go grab a beer, breathe some air, empty my head. Watch the store for me?"

"I got you, boss," Ahab said. "Get out. Go."

Max mouthed a silent "Bravo!" and headed for the door.

From a seat on his front stoop, Max executed the first step in his rescue plan: call Tina Falcone.

Tina had been his side partner during his eight-year tour with Manhattan South Homicide, and he'd worked with her on a couple of tabloid-grabbing multiples after he'd quit the force and gone private. He and she came from two widely spaced islands in the city's ethnic and sexual archipelago, a straight Jew and a gay Sicilian; they were, in her coinage, Butch Calamari and the Sundance Yid. But they had bonded in their time together pushing an NYPD-issue Crown Vic on the trail of bad guys with bloodied knives and smoking guns. When she called Max her guru, she meant it. When he called Tina the best murder police in the department, he meant that too.

"The Sundance Yid!" she exclaimed, hearing his voice. "Whatchu been up to? You couldn't call your old sidekick? Couldn't even send a postcard—'Hey, girlfriend, how ya doin'?' What, you don't love old Butchie anymore?"

She laughed. He didn't.

"We still partners?" he asked.

"Always, Dance—you know that," she said. "You okay? You don't sound so good."

"I don't feel so good. Why I'm calling."

"What, you into one of your situations?"

"That's exactly what I've got, and it's a bad one. Can we talk?"

"So talk."

"No, I mean can you get away for maybe a half hour?"

"Yeah, I guess so. I'm just sitting around here waiting to catch a case is all. Your place?"

"No, can't be there—I'll explain why when I see you. Posto okay with you?"

"Sure, Dance. What, fifteen minutes?"

"That'll work," Max said. "Thanks, T. See you there."

CHAPTER 5

The Walls Have Ears

Max was still on the stoop, killing a few minutes till Tina time, when Ahab emerged from the office and took a seat beside him.

"What's with the sweater, kid?" Max said. "It's May Day. Spring is in the air. You're sitting here—enjoy the sun."

Ahab was wearing a black hoodie with *CCNY* in block letters on one sleeve; he'd spent a bored year and a half there before becoming a cop. He raised the hem a couple of inches, letting Max glimpse the Walther PPX tucked into his waistband.

"You're tooled up," Max said. "How come?"

"See that sketchy-looking dude on the northeast corner? Heavy-set mope on the cell phone, in the silver suit? Leaning on the black Suburban?"

Max glanced that way and shrugged. "Yeah, I see him," he said. "Guy on a cell, ass parked on his car—what's sketchy about that?"

"Well, one thing, he's been there since I got here this morning, looking this way a lot."

"Yeah, and?"

"The way he keeps waving that hand every which of a way? Looks like some ginzo shit to me."

"Slow down, man," Max said. "This is New York. Case you haven't noticed, we all talk with our hands, even on cell calls, when the one we're talking to can't see. Welcome to Ethnic City."

"Yeah, I know, I know," Ahab said, "but like we used to say in my piece of Ethnic City, over Bed-Stuy, the shit ain't right. I think he's one of the Beak's boys, and I think he's here to make sure you don't go anywhere you shouldn't oughta go. Like the One-Three house. Or Manhattan South. Or maybe a sit-down with a reporter."

"So I'm supposed to stay on lockdown in my own home?"

"I can go mess with him if you want. Keep him busy and give you a head start case he's here to tail you."

Max thought about that for a moment. "No, bro, let the hump tail me," he said, "but buzz me if he does, so I know. I've got a zig-out I think will work."

Ahab nodded. Max crossed Eighteenth Street and headed up Third Avenue, timing his gait to brush through one of the mope's more operatic hand gestures. He'd covered about half a block, when his BlackBerry vibrated in his pocket.

"You got company," Ahab said.

"I figured," Max replied.

He kept ambling up Third to Twenty-First Street and then headed right, in the direction of the NYPD's Thirteenth Precinct station house. The One-Three squad had been his first billet as a young, newly minted detective third grade, and he was well acquainted with the folkways of cops on a sunny day in a quiet precinct; they liked to hang on the sidewalk, have a smoke, and bitch about the bosses and the demands for more and more summonses. He figured he'd see somebody he knew, and he did, an old-timer named Harry Something-or-Other; remembering names was not one of Max's gifts.

"Hey, buddy," he said, clapping a hand on Harry's shoulder, "long time no see. How they hangin'?"

"Well, fuck me if it ain't Max fucking Christian. Hey, guys," he called to a couple of young detectives lounging against the side of an emergency services truck, "come meet a real-life case-closing NYPD legend. In his own mind anyway—what kinda legend puts in his papers before he puts in his years?"

Harry guffawed. Max shook some hands and exchanged some smiles, thinking how young the newbies all looked—or maybe just how old he felt in their company.

"Listen, guys," he said. "I could use a favor."

"Sure, man," Harry said, "anything—long as it doesn't get the rat squad on our ass."

"I'm working a marital," Max said, "and the guy I'm tailing has put a tail on me. The guy in the silver suit, leaning on that RMP halfway up the block—see him? Used to be we were more protective of our blue-and-whites than that."

"Yeah," Harry said, "I see the skel. You need us to hassle him a little?"

"Just enough to slow his progress so I can lose his ass. Normally, I'd say fuck it. I'm in the game; he's in the game—next case, it could me tailing him. But I'm headed for a meet with my client, and I'd just as soon he wasn't around listening in."

"We got your back, Max," Harry said. "We'll ticket him for loitering, what with the bosses being all into quality-of-life crimes."

"Again?"

"Again. Thanks, Mayor de Blasio."

Max laughed. "Thanks, buddy," he said. "You ever suspect your wife of wandering, call me—I'll handle it for free."

"'Preciate the offer, buddy, but you're too late. She wandered, I wandered, and we're divorced—case closed. But you could buy me a couple rounds at Plug Uglies sometime if you're of a mind to."

"Done," Max said, already in motion toward Second Avenue. When he peeked back, the guy in the silver suit was haranguing two detectives while a uniform stood apart, writing a summons.

Posto was a smallish neighborhood bistro specializing in thin-crust pizza, but it served a wide range of Max's needs: it was his restaurant when he was hungry, his snack bar when he wasn't, his rendezvous room when he needed to get with someone under the radar, and his ashram when he felt overwhelmed by solitude and self-pity. It was his regular meeting place with Tina, whether it was a case or simply their close friendship that brought them together.

He found her waiting in their favorite booth when he arrived—a vantage point from which she could watch the front entrance and he could see the side door. She rose to greet him, dressed, as always, in black from her blazer to her slim jeans to her bit loafers; even her eyes looked like pools of liquefied onyx. He gave her a peck on the cheek, but her smile chilled to a frown when he slid into the seat opposite hers.

"You look like shit, Dance," she said. "You're rich, you're smart, and you're handsome—well, sort of handsome, if you're into guys, which I'm not. Things can't be as bad as you look right now."

"Things are worse than bad, T. Trust me. That's why I called you."

"What, Dance? Talk. Tell Mama T."

"I can't unless I have your word it stays at this table. You can't repeat it to anyone—no cops, no bosses, not your buddy at the Bureau. Nobody."

"Not even Cloudy?"

"Not even Cloudy. I know she's your wife, but she's also a lawyer, an officer of the court. This once, this one time, no pillow talk."

Their drinks arrived, a tumbler of barbera for Max and a Diet Coke for Tina. He felt her studying him across the rim of her glass.

"You up to something bad, partner?" she asked.

"No. Not now anyway. I may have to be later."

"You know I play by the rules, Max. I don't color outside the lines."

"I know that, T. I'm reaching out to you because I'm desperate. I need your help, and if I color outside the lines, I'll surrender to you before my SIG stops smoking. I just need you to keep what I'm about to tell you to yourself for a little bit."

"A little bit? How long's that?"

"Ten days. Two weeks max. Maybe less."

"Jesus, Dance, you're my best friend except for Cloudy, but if this is any kind of serious shit, you're asking a lot."

"I know, T. I had to ask." He sipped his barbera. "You can say no."

Silence fell like a curtain between them. Max drained his glass and held up his empty for another.

"Let me get one of those too," Tina said.

"I've never seen you drink on duty, girl," Max said.

"I figured I needed to this once. If they had real drinks here, I'd say fuck the book and have one."

"How come?"

"'Cause I'm about to do something deeply stupid."

"Meaning?"

"Meaning I'm buying your deal sight unseen, which puts my whole career at risk. I hope not for nothing."

Max hoisted his glass and took a deep draft, hoping for a calm that didn't come. "Charlie Beak has my son," he said.

"He fucking what?"

"His hoods kidnapped Jay on the Penn campus in broad daylight. He wants twenty-five mil—two-point-five a day for ten days—if we want him back alive and well."

"That's fucked up big-time, Dance. What're you gonna do?"

"Pay him. Dew has the money, no problem, and for now, we've got no other option."

"Damn, Dance, you used to be murder police. You know the odds against getting the vic back alive, whether you pay up or not."

"I know," Max said. "That's why I'm trying to figure a way to bust him out before the last payday."

"Dance, baby, I hate to break it to you, but you ain't Batman, and your boy wonder Ahab ain't Robin. I mean, it hurts to even think it, but how do you even know if Jay's still alive?"

"He was as of this morning. The Beak let Dew and me see him for a few minutes on Skype."

"And?"

"He was okay. Scared but okay. But remember what your Bureau buddy told you once? 'Charlie Beak is a student of pain?'"

"Yeah, I remember. It sounded at the time like he was being a little—what? Melodramatic, I guess."

"Well, it turns out it's true. Fucking creep told me so himself. Said pain is the only way to pleasure. His pleasure anyway, and now he's got Jay to play with."

Tina drank some wine, set the glass down, and wiped up a ring on the table with a paper napkin. "You should've reported this on day one, Dance," she said. "To the Bureau, if not us. The *federales* have resources we don't have."

"'Call the cops, the boy dies' is essentially what the Beak told me. I couldn't risk it—the guy owns enough cops to know if I report it. It's gotta be me gets Jay out."

"All by your lonesome? You're fucking kidding, right?"

"I've got friends who don't play by the book like you, T," Max said. "Some of 'em don't even know there's a book to be played by."

"Yeah, and Charlie Beak's got soldiers out the wazoo. Plus he's smart—he's not one of these half-cooked zips just off the plane from Palermo."

Max polished off his second barbera and raised his empty again for a refill. "I know," he said.

"You know and don't fucking care?" Tina said. "What are you, some kind of crazy?"

"I have no choice. I want my son back, and I want the Beak dead."

Tina stared at him as if he were a stranger. "You better make sure it's self-defense, Dance," she said. "You just copped to premeditation, and I don't want to be the one locks you up for murder one."

Max laughed an impersonation of a laugh. "Mitigating circumstances," he said. "He kidnapped my son, and he's the biggest drug trafficker in New York. Most you could charge

45

would be manslaughter one, and I doubt you could make it stick."

"I don't want any part of any killing, justified or not."

"I know. I'd never ask that."

"So why are we here? What's my part in this movie?"

"First of all, I need someone I can talk to."

"That would be Meridew. Last I checked, she's still your wife and Jay's mom, and from what you're saying, she's also the one writing the ransom checks."

"You know what I'm saying, T—I need someone who knows me and knows the street. All those years in that Crown Vic? I spent more time with you than I did with Dew, and she didn't even need to get jealous. I mean, given your off-brand sexuality."

Tina managed a smile. "So what do you want me to do, besides be your buddy and pal?"

"I need to figure out where the hell Jay is. You remember Matt Mullarkey?"

"Yeah, sort of. He was that hairbag used to be in the tech unit? TARU?"

"Charter member, yeah. He does jobs for me now—me and a couple of other PIs. He's got gizmos at home that the TARU guys never dreamed of, but so far, he can't trace that Skype call this morning. All he's sure of, it wasn't from Lido Beach."

"The Beak's been in Lido like forever. Mullarkey's sure?"

"He's sure. His words: 'The compass points north.' Maybe uptown, maybe north Bronx, maybe Westchester, or maybe farther. Just not Lido or anywhere else on the island."

"And add unlawful flight to his RICO case if he's even in Jersey? I don't think so."

"Or it could be he's lying low while his mopes are trying to hunt down I. M. Trubble."

"The former drug prince of Central Harlem?"

"Yeah, him," Max said. "You prob'ly heard he got RICO'd too, but the feds flipped him and put him in WitPro. You can bet the Beak's put out a contract on him. Take him out, you gut the case."

"They gotta have him stashed somewhere," Tina said, "like

on a military base or somewhere. I mean, there's a reason they call it witness protection."

"Yeah, but the Beak doesn't look to me like a guy who gives up easily, and the feds aren't quite as incorruptible as they'd like us to think."

"Sounds like you think a lot of Beaky's tradecraft."

"Let's say I think a lot of his cunning," Max said. "Remember lesson number one in *our* tradecraft?"

"I remember it well, sensei," Tina answered with a mock precocious schoolgirl smile. "Lesson number one: never underestimate the bad guys."

"Good, grasshopper. I'm hungry. You got time for a slice?"

Tina pushed up her blazer sleeve, glanced at her watch, and shook her head. "Naw, it's tempting, but I should get back to the shop. Let me guess what you need me to do—ask around to see if I can find out where he bunks, right?"

"Right. Exactly. Just don't give up why you're asking."

"I do know a gal, Cindy, in OCCB—that's Organized Crime, case you forgot. She and I hung out some back in the BC times."

"BC?" Max said. "Let me guess. Before Cloudy?"

"You're smarter than you look, sensei. My loving wife doesn't like thinking I even have a past."

"Mine doesn't either. But this Cindy—she know stuff?"

"She knows everything. The boys don't put her on the street, 'cause she's a girl, but she knows what's in those computers and those filing cabinets. The guys need two and two put together, they come to her. I'll see what she's got. Her and my FBI buddy—my two best bets."

"You got him out of the closet yet?"

Tina laughed. "Pretty much, except at the office. The Bureau's come a long way since Edgar and Clyde were the only ones allowed to be gay, but they're still kinda primitive over there."

"And what about *your* hairbag in the One-Three? The king of the paper chasers?"

"Digger Calhoun? He's retired, but he might take this as a one-off if you made it worth his while."

"Used to be an accidental-on-purpose titty rub from you would set him in motion."

"Stopped working after he turned sixty-five," Tina said. "But he can still chase paper better than anyone in the whole NYPD. I'll sound him out."

"Discreetly," Max said.

"Discreetly goes for you too. I could lose my gun and shield if it got out why I was asking so many questions."

Max reached across the table and took her hand. "I owe you, girlfriend," he said. "I owe you, and I love you."

"Easy on the love stuff," she said. "Cloudy'd go all stormy on my white ass if she heard you talking that smack to me."

"Couldn't help myself," he said.

"Oh," she said, "and will you get that fucking ear fixed? It's nasty just looking at it. What's it been—three, four years?"

Max touched what remained of his right ear. The lower third was still missing. "Not time yet," he said.

"Why not?"

"You'll recall it was the Beak's late, unlamented hitter Joey Primitivo who shot it off. Every time I shave in the morning, it's a reminder."

"Reminder of what?" Tina asked.

"That it's payback time," Max said.

Max took a roundabout route back to the office, thinking about what else he saw in the mirror every morning. The image looking back at him told him things he didn't like admitting even to himself. It told him that he wasn't young anymore—that he was kidding himself thinking that anyone still saw him as that precociously street-smart boy detective on the One-Three squad. Dark quarter-moons had formed below his eyes. A couple of spider veins had lately etched his Roman nose, in spite of his many months of reined-in drinking. He'd kept his mop of curly dark hair, but the silver threads were multiplying like a metastatic cancer. The days when people called him handsome and meant it were behind him; now they said he was "showing his age" behind his back, and they said, "You're looking well," to his face. He saw the man he felt himself becoming—a burned-out case, a hermit too long withdrawn from the life of the world.

He stopped at Barfly on his way home for a beer he didn't need. Verna, the sassy Filipina American behind the bar, set a PBR in front of him and asked how he was doing. He mumbled an "Okay," but his eyes and mind were on the street outside, reassuring him that the guy on his tail had given up.

It was pushing three o'clock when he got back to his office and found the New New Girl playing FreeCell on her computer. She was a tawny beauty with dreams of being a model; she'd been on Max's to-do list before Meridew's arrival from Gladwyne.

"So what's with the blinds, kid?" he asked. *Kid* was his generic term of address for the succession of temps who worked for him; he tended to forget their names, even when they'd graced his bed.

"What about the blinds?" she answered, not looking up from her game.

"They're all drawn. I thought I mentioned I like daylight. What's up?"

She shrugged. "I dunno," she said. "Ask Ahab. Was his idea, not mine."

Max walked back and asked Ahab. "It's all good, boss," Ahab said, but as soon as the words were out, he winked and gestured toward the stairs.

Max followed him up to the living room. "Meridew here?" he asked.

"No, she had to go back to Philly," Ahab said. "She said to tell you there's some kind of tangle with the money piece, and her friend Edith's flying in from Paris to get it untangled."

"So what's with the blinds? And why are we upstairs?"

"Jamie? Mullarkey's li'l' brother?"

"Yeah? He find anything?"

"Yeah. In fact, he found two things. Turns out you were right, chief. Big Brother been listening in on us—downstairs anyway."

49

"And pulling down the blinds is supposed to protect us? C'mon."

"From gizmo one, yeah. It's a laser mic."

"Which is?"

"It's a thing where you point a laser at a window from across the street, say, and it picks up everything said inside," Ahab said. "You need tech specs past that, talk to Jamie—I'm not your man. He says the reception isn't great, but they can get enough to figure out what we're up to."

"We know where the laser's coming from?"

"I walked over there while you were out—the high-rise the color of vomit—and asked the super if anybody new'd moved in the last week or so. He said, in fact, yeah. Said there's some business guy from Brazil bought a second-floor condo over there to use when he's in town. Which, it turns out, is a month or two out of the year. Rest of the time, he rents it out, and two new guys just moved in."

"Anyone we know?"

"One of them answers the description of the corner lookout who was on your tail. Super said the other guy looked half hippie, half nerdy. Super says they brought in a shitload of stuff for a short-stay rental."

Max stepped to the window and scanned the second floor.

"You can't necessarily see 'em, boss," Ahab said. "They don't have to be right in the window. What Jamie says anyway."

"So what do we do?"

"Jamie said he could come by tomorrow with some high-tech *Star Wars* shit that can fuck up the laser for real, if you really need the blinds back up."

"Mmp," Max said. "Sounds like a plan to me."

"Hold on, boss—wait'll you've heard about gizmo number two. Which two chumps calling themselves detectives walk past every day and never noticed. I'm talking about us if you haven't guessed."

"And I'm supposed to read your mind? C'mon with it."

"It's a microwave transmitter. Beak's boys must've come by in the wee hours and stuck it up right over one of your office windows. According to Jamie, it can hear through walls twenty inches thick. He says it can pick up everything in your office and maybe mine. Oh, and the reception area, 'case they want to hear our trusty gatekeeper filing her nails."

"Jesus," Max said. "Does it pop corn too?" He stood and ran his fingers through his thicket of kinks and curls. "Can I pour you a drink?" he said. "The book doesn't apply upstairs. You're a guest in my home."

"No, thanks," Ahab said. "Check that—yeah, maybe I will. You got scotch?"

"Yeah," Max said. He poured a Chivas for Ahab and a straight Mount Gay for himself and set them on the coffee table between them. "So what are we supposed to do?"

"Jamie's suggestion—and I think it's a good one—is to keep the blinds down. Let 'em think we're on to the laser but not the microwave. Anything about Jay, we discuss up here— Jamie did a sweep, and it's clean. Your office, we talk smack, like we just did before you went out. Make 'em believe we're chasing our tails."

Max lay back in his favorite corner of the couch, cradling his drink on his belly. A long moment passed in silence.

"Jamie's right; you're right," he said, sitting straight up. "As of now, this is the war room. Downstairs is the theater of the absurd."

CHAPTER 6

Houston, We've Got a Problem

Three days had passed—three empty, endless days with no word, no news, and no fresh intel—when the Beak rang the private line Max had set up for him. "It's your friend Don Carlo," his unmistakable voice said. "It's time we met again."

"You're not my friend, motherfucker," Max said. "One day soon, you'll know that. It could be your dying thought."

"Again, I should caution you against empty threats," the Beak said. "My men will come for you promptly at ten thirty. Please be outside your office when they arrive. Oh, and this time, be so kind as to come unarmed."

"What, I'm supposed to trust you? The sleazebag who snatched my son? I don't think so."

"Suit yourself," the Beak replied, "but if you do bring a weapon, it will be confiscated for the duration of our meeting and returned to you, empty, upon your return home. My agenda is strictly business. I guarantee your safety, and in any case, I abhor bloodshed."

"Except when you inflict it? As a student of pain?"

"Let me amend my remark, Detective. I abhor bloodshed when it might draw the undue attention of the police, as the death of one of their honored alumni surely would. Which in turn would endanger my fragile peace with our city's other four borgatas. They, regrettably, are already quite jealous of my success."

"They've failed at rat-proofing, and you haven't?"

"Not until now," the Beak said. "May I count on seeing you shortly?"

"Will I see my son?"

"Perhaps, perhaps not—I haven't decided yet. In either case, you have my word that he is unharmed."

"Yeah, right," Max said, and he abruptly hung up; he had no stomach for the politesse of exchanging goodbyes.

"That him, boss?" Ahab asked, looming in the doorway.

"That was him," Max said. "He's sending his boys to pick me up here at ten thirty."

They headed upstairs to the war room.

"We gonna wire you up?" Ahab asked when they were seated.

"I'll wear Mullarkey's magic glasses and hope they work wherever I'm going. They find a body mic on me, they'll punish me by putting Jay back in the box."

"The Beak's latest theorem of pain? Hurt the dad by hurting the son?"

"Exactly."

"Y'know, boss," Ahab said, "there are places to hide a body mic where mopes like them don't like to go."

"They searched me once," Max said. "They go everywhere."

"Except the glasses?"

"Except the glasses. The mic's in the bridge, but I don't know how much range it has."

"I've got Mullarkey coming down here with his stuff. We'll tail you. My boy Death is gonna ride with us for muscle."

"Right. Just don't be obvious."

"C'mon, boss. I didn't survive three years as a narco undercover being obvious."

Max smiled. "Forgive me, Officer," he said. "I misspoke."

Max was sitting out on the stoop when a black Escalade with dark-tinted windows pulled up on the dot of ten thirty. The rear door on the passenger's side swung open. Max bent for a look and saw the Beak's man Il Lupo waving him in.

He hesitated.

"Whaddya—some kinda pussy?" Il Lupo growled. "We was here to hurt you, you'd be over Bellevue on life support right now. Get in the fucking truck before we change our mind. The don don't take kind to people get called in and they RSVP no."

Max squeezed into the back seat in what little space Il Lupo's 350-pound bulk allowed him and submitted to a heavy-handed body search. The pat-down yielded up not just his SIG but also his cell phone.

Il Lupo pocketed them both. "You'll get 'em back when the don says you can have 'em back. Now lemme see them glasses."

"Why?" Max said. "I need them."

"Fuck what you need. You gonna give 'em up, or you gonna be a hard case over here and make me take 'em?"

"Take 'em," Max said.

Il Lupo snatched them up and handed them forward to a young man with streaked blond hair tied back in a ponytail. He wore a black sateen Chemical Brothers All-UK Tour jacket, and it occurred to Max that he could be the nerdy hippie partner in the duo manning the Beak's listening post across Eighteenth Street. The kid scrutinized the glasses through his own rimless Ben Franklins and touched the pinhole opening to the mic concealed in the bridge.

"Cute," he said.

"Thanks, neighbor," Max replied, hoping to get a rise. He didn't; the nerdy hippie ignored him, which told Max his hunch was right, and stowed the glasses in the glove box. "I think we'd best keep these for now," he said. "Let's roll."

I'm fucked, Max thought as the Escalade pulled away from the curb and headed east toward—

Toward what?

He couldn't tell; they had barely made it past Second

Avenue, when a black hood came down over his eyes and blotted out the streetscape.

I'm truly fucked, he thought.

"Lose that gray Malibu hanging two or three cars behind us," the nerdy hippie said, his smirk audible in his voice. "He's tailing us."

I'm truly, totally, nonconsensually fucked.

Blinded by the hood, he tried being his own GPS tracker, but the wheelman was good at his trade; his zigs and zags overwhelmed Max's calculations before they'd detoured around Times Square.

"The tail still on us?" Il Lupo asked.

"Naw, we shook him somewhere around South Street Seaport," the driver said. "Or maybe it was down by the High Line. Fuck, I ain't a tour guide. I don't work off no map. I just drive."

"Yeah, well," Il Lupo said, "keep driving like you been driving. This *strunz* been in the papers, all about being a smart cop. We'll see how fucking smart he is, trying to figure where the fuck he's at."

Houston, we've got a problem, Max thought. *I've run out of lifelines. I'm in deep space, and I'm fucking lost.*

"Welcome, Detective," the Beak said, waving Max to a seat across the desk, "and please accept my apologies for the, ah, security measures involved in bringing you here. I hope my men have not been unduly brusque with you."

"Fuck them, and fuck you," Max said. "Where's my son?"

"Again, my apologies. He is not here. This is my workplace— or, rather, one of them—and workplaces are for business. Your son is at my home, under my protection, enjoying my hospitality. He's doubtless at his books now—he is quite the diligent student, as my own son was. You must be quite proud."

"I am, but I want him at my home, under my protection," Max said. "And I want him unharmed."

"As I've pledged will be the case, so long as you and Signora Christian continue to meet my terms."

They were sitting in a small, sparsely furnished office that was pitch dark except for a single klieg lamp set in the ceiling. It bathed Charlie Beak in a circle of brilliant light, leaving Max a secondary presence half hidden in the surrounding blackness.

"Pretty theatrical," he said.

"Not my taste, I assure you," the Beak said. "This venue is a recent acquisition from somebody of a more flamboyant nature than my own. It is, in that sense, a fixer-upper, but my son thought it was a good buy, both from an investment and a marketing standpoint. I trust his judgment completely."

The two men sat studying one another in silence, each waiting for the other's next move. "Once again, my apologies," the Beak said finally. "I have been a neglectful host. May I offer you something to drink? A Mount Gay rum perhaps? Straight up?"

Max nodded. *Jesus*, he thought, *they did their research. They know my warm-weather drink. What the fuck else do they know about me?*

The Beak gestured to a flunky standing barely visible in a dark corner, waiting for his cue. "A Mount Gay neat for Mr. Christian and an anisette for me."

The drinks appeared. The Beak took a discreet sip. Max took a greedy swallow.

"And you've called this meeting because?" he asked.

The Beak planted his elbows on the desk and rested his chin on the tips of his steepled fingers. "Because for the second time in the past four days, your payment to my account in Vanuatu is overdue," he said. "That is quite unfortunate for both of us. And could be, prospectively, for your son."

"There's been some kind of glitch at my wife's bank. She's been in Philadelphia all week, trying to straighten it out, and a friend who's a major shareholder in the bank has flown in from Paris to help."

"That would be the widow Clift, I suppose. I had business

dealings with her late husband, as you doubtless know. How generous of her to tear herself away from her lover—"

"Her fiancé," Max said.

"As you wish. I'm quite old-fashioned in these matters. You're confident the issues can be put to rest?"

"Completely confident," Max said, "and we're prepared to pay the vig you've demanded."

"No. To show that I'm not a heartless man, I've decided not to require the penalty payments, nor will I punish your son for your delinquency. On your word, of course, that what you call a glitch can be resolved."

"I'm overwhelmed by your generosity," Max said with a dry smile. "I mean, you being a student of pain and all."

"You owe my son your gratitude. It was he who persuaded me that patience would be better for business than pain in the present situation, given that your payments have otherwise arrived in a timely way."

"Patience over pain? Sounds like the apple fell pretty far from the tree."

"Not at all, Detective," the Beak said, smiling. "Luca is quite like me, but he's been schooled in modern business practices, and he's persuaded me that pain is only one business strategy among many. If I understand your history correctly, that would be your belief as well."

"If you're asking me whether I've inflicted pain in my work, the answer is yes, I have, and I will. But I'm not like you. I take no pleasure in it. Or let me amend that: it would give me great pleasure to hurt you if you inflict any more pain on my son."

The Beak laughed. "Oh please," he said. "Your son's penalty for acting out during our Skype conversation the other day was to have been thirty minutes—a mere thirty minutes—in the little-ease. I had to extract him after eighteen he was wailing so loudly."

"You hurt him again, I'll—"

"You'll what, Detective? Need I again remind you who holds the cards in this game? Your son's well-being will depend on your cooperation and his behavior, not on empty threats."

"You do hold the cards now," Max said, "but I have a long memory and a short fuse."

"There will be no need for me to punish him so long as you continue paying down your debt to me. I take no pleasure in tormenting someone with so low a threshold of pain. I would suggest, if I may, that such fragility is the mark of a sheltered childhood."

"You can say that? As a father?"

"My son, Detective, endured twelve hours in the little-ease in his teens without so much as a whimper."

"What'd he do? Raid the cookie jar? Smoke a joint?"

"He got an underage girl in trouble, as they say. Not just any girl, a Sicilian girl, and not just any Sicilian girl—she was the daughter of one of my capos. Her father demanded punishment and was allowed, at my invitation, to witness it. And of course, my son married the girl."

"And they've lived happily ever after?"

The Beak paused for a sip of anisette. "So far as a parent can tell, yes," he said. "Elena is not nearly so educated as my Luca, but she is quite pretty and very fertile—she's blessed me with two grandsons and a granddaughter, and she's not yet twenty-two."

"And your son has a *goomar*? A little something on the side?"

"The correct term is *coumare,* Detective, and the answer is no. If he did, he would be in violation of a new code of conduct he wrote himself and would be subject to appropriate punishment. We no longer tolerate taking mistresses in our organization. The Paolucci borgata honors its women."

"Cheating is a sin? How abstemious."

"We defer to Holy Mother Church to decide what is or isn't sinful. For us, fidelity is a business principle, one we enforce. A man who cannot keep his marriage vows is—" The Beak paused.

"A security risk?" Max asked.

"Precisely. How can such a man be trusted to keep his vows to our family if he cannot be true to his own?"

"So," Max said, his eyes widening, "am I hearing right? You

let your son write a code of conduct for men who were made when he was in Pampers?"

"Yes, and marital fidelity was not the only new requirement. The code also imposes limits on weight and more conservative rules on business dress. Fat men in shiny suits and pinkie rings are offensive to my eye and my son's."

"It looks to me like your man Il Lupo didn't get that memo. He's gotta be three hundred, maybe three fifty, and his pinkie's carrying a diamond as big as the Ritz."

"As Scott Fitzgerald once put it," the Beak said. "Nice allusion, Detective. But to answer your question, such lifestyle changes are hard to impose on our older soldiers. Changing a culture is never easy, but Luca has been quite insistent that it must begin. If we are a business, he says, our people must look like businessmen, not like extras from *The Sopranos*."

"I thought the don was the law in all such matters," Max said.

"The don was and is the law, but typically, he rules in consultation with his counselor, his *consigliere*. That is my son's role in our organization—although, again at his suggestion, we've changed the nomenclature quite a bit."

"To?"

"To—how should I respond when I'm still getting used to the new language myself? On our new table of organization, I am the chairman and CEO of our umbrella company, Agnese Worldwide Enterprises, and Luca is my executive vice president. The old honorifics die hard, and most of my men—the older men, certainly—still think of me as the boss or the don. But those titles have been tainted by our debased popular culture, and my Luca has persuaded me that they are obsolete."

"You've really placed a lot of faith in your son's counsel," Max said.

"Total faith, Detective. I've placed him on the highest branch of my succession tree."

"Whatever the fuck that is. Excuse the language."

"You'll find me quite forgiving of small offenses, Detective," the Beak said, though there was little suggesting forgiveness in his smile. "Like any modern corporation, we try to plan ahead for contingencies. We don't wait until one of our executives disappears or dies—we rank them in advance, strictly on their performance, so that we have an order of succession in place when an opening occurs. The chart depicting that order vaguely resembles a tree. Hence, a succession tree."

"Sounds pretty corporate," Max said. "Bet it cuts down on the gunplay, though, if everybody knows who's next for what job."

"Indeed. Since we instituted planned lines of succession, our internal casualty count has been near zero. May I offer you another drink?"

"I could be persuaded."

In a heartbeat, a second Mount Gay was in front of him. *Fuckers not only know my drink*, he thought, *but they know how fast I want it.* "You're clearly one well-educated motherfucker," he said, "but what's with all the boardroom jargon? I thought your son was the one with the MBA."

"As indeed he is. I never imagined him becoming part of all this. I never wanted it. I wanted something better for him—something cleaner, something less dangerous. Life, in what we men of honor call this thing of ours, can be nasty, brutish, and short."

"Hobbesian?" Max asked.

"Exactly, Detective. I see that you too are an educated man—it's not often one meets a police officer acquainted even with Fitzgerald, let alone Hobbes. My business, my life's work, is indeed Hobbesian." He held up his hands, palms forward, as if assessing his manicure. "This Cosa Nostra, this thing of ours, is dying—dying of internal rot and rampant betrayal. The difference between me and my fellow dons is that I know we are in the end time of the old ways and am adapting to it. I am, thus far, a survivor, and I intend to remain one."

"A survivor with a RICO indictment hanging over your head," Max said, "and an informer prepared to tattle on you."

"Just so, and if I cannot persuade or compel the Reverend Trubble to hold his tongue, I could be joining several of my peers as guests of the government. Were you aware, Detective, that half of the other New York borgatas are managed today by acting bosses while their leaders languish in prison? I would hate for my son to be thrust too soon into that role."

The Beak smiled a smile Max hadn't seen before. He'd seen chilling, he'd seen sardonic, and he'd seen self-satisfied, but this smile was different. It was wistful, and it took the Beak a minute and a deeper sip of anisette to resume.

"It was never my plan to involve Luca in the family business, Detective," he said. "Indeed, I sent him across America to Stanford to get him as far from my world as I could."

"As Don Vito Corleone tried to shelter Michael by sending him off to college?" Max said. "This is beginning to sound like the script for *The Godfather.*"

Again, the wistful smile appeared, and the Beak took a sip of anisette. "I suppose you could say that," he said, "except that there's a role reversal in our situation. It is the father who has Michael's ruthlessness and the son who has Don Vito's wisdom."

"And you made him your successor in a life you know is doomed? Maybe end up in a cell next to his dad's in supermax, locked down twenty-three hours a day? I'd say yeah, that qualifies as ruthless."

"Trust me, Detective. I did try for a quite different outcome. My graduation gift to Luca was a hedge fund—or, more accurately, the start-up money required to launch one. The design was his own, a student project at Stanford. His faculty adviser called it a work of genius, and so it's turned out to be. Four years out of school, and he's more than halfway to his first billion dollars."

"Laundering Daddy's drug money?"

"I am an investor, if that's what you're asking, but I'm by no means the only one. The prospect of wealth is an opiate more powerful than any I'm falsely accused of selling. Several of my son's prime clients are rival hedge fund managers, hoping, I suppose, to learn from the boy genius in their midst."

Max drank off the last of his Mount Gay. Another was at his elbow in less than a minute. "And yet you've crowned him prince of your tottering empire? When he could be what passes on Wall Street for legit?"

The wistful smile flashed on again and this time lingered. "You're a father," the Beak said. "You know how sons are— how headstrong, how rebellious they can be."

"Yeah," Max said, returning the wistful smile. "My boy wants to be a political hack, plus a basketball bum like his dad, and neither his mom nor I can talk him out of either one."

"So you can understand my situation," the Beak said. "Tell me, Detective—can I possibly invite you to stay for lunch? The kitchen in this place is smallish, but my chef is quite clever. He can conjure up some pasta with pesto if that suits you and a quite decent red. Will you stay?"

"Why the fuck are you even asking?" Max asked. "For all I know, you might kidnap me too. Stuff me in your little-ease and hit my wife for another twenty-five mil—which, given the state of our marriage, she might not be quite so eager to pay."

"Why? Because, Detective, I've enjoyed our conversation, and if you'll indulge me, I'd like to keep it going awhile longer. You have every reason to hate me; I understand that. But beneath your tough-guy attitude and your often coarse language, I sense a civilized man, and there are not many such men in my world. Or yours, I might venture to guess."

Max was a man of instincts, and his first was to say no: you don't break bread with your enemy. But everything he'd learned about interrogation as a cop held that if a suspect said word one, you should keep him talking—you just might hear something you don't know.

"Yeah, I'll do lunch," he said.

What the fuck? he thought. *All this daddy-to-daddy sentimentality just might be an opening to an alternate route home.*

CHAPTER 7

Fathers and Sons

"My son, God help us both, has a real genius for this business," the Beak said, twirling a coil of linguine al pesto deftly onto his fork. "I truly believe he could be the first real visionary in our world since Charles Luciano, may his soul rest in peace."

"Lucky fucking Luciano?" Max replied. "A visionary? Based on everything I've read or heard, he was a stone-cold killer."

"That's how he came to power, yes, Detective. Wars were then a sad and costly part of the life our fathers and grandfathers imported to these shores. But all that took place before Luciano founded the Commission that oversees our affairs and resolves our disputes before they lead to war."

"By deciding who does or doesn't need to get dead—what I understand anyway."

"I suppose that has sometimes been the case, yes. But tell me, my friend—is not the sanctioned sacrifice of one or two lives preferable to the loss of many in a war that profits no one? The days of going to the mattresses are happily behind us, thanks to Luciano's foresight."

"Killing is killing, wholesale or retail," Max said. "From a homicide cop's perspective, anyway. One wise guy popped another, we didn't shed any tears—we just called it thinning the herd. Oh, and by the way, I may be enjoying your pasta and your wine, but I'm not your friend."

"Pity," the Beak said, "when I've been so enjoying your company." He paused for a sip of red from a delicate gold-rimmed glass. "A Lamoresco from Sicily. Rather good, don't you think?"

"It's okay," Max said, "but you were saying?"

"I was saying that the formation of that Commission was our first tentative step out of our bloody provincial past into the ways of a modern corporate world. Thus, my view of Luciano as a visionary."

"And you hope your Luca will take the next step?"

"It isn't a matter of hope, Detective," the Beak said. "It is a matter of certainty. The revolution has already begun within the Paolucci borgata. The other families will follow, or they will die."

"And Luca will be the boss of bosses? The *capo di tutti capi*?"

The Beak's answering laugh had the sound of shattering glass. "There is no such animal now," he said, "and there can be no such animal in the future—not in the time of RICO. We are all under siege, as I myself can attest. For the five families to be seen as part of a single entity with a single leader would only multiply the dangers to each of us under that fascistic law. No, Detective, that is not my vision for Luca, and it is not his for himself."

The Beak paused and snapped his fingers at the flunky in the shadows. "Signore Christian's glass is empty," he said. "He is my guest. That should not happen."

"Sorry, boss," the flunky said, bounding forward to pour a refill.

"'Boss?'" Max said, taking a grateful swallow. "Sounds like not everyone has learned the new nomenclature."

"Turning a battleship is never easy, Detective," the Beak said. "Ask your former bosses at One Police Plaza adapting to a new mayor, a new commissioner, and new theories on combating crime."

"And you believe your son can turn your battleship? A boy

not yet out of his twenties? A boy with no real experience in the life?"

"He grew up in the life, in the constant company of rough and vulgar men. Four of my best soldiers were his security team at Deerfield and Stanford. He's been privy to every detail of my business, every number on my books. He's been preparing my tax returns flawlessly since he was eighteen. So yes, Detective, I have great faith in his ability to create a new business model for the Paolucci borgata—one that will ensure our survival in these trying times."

"What, by taking the business legitimate?" Max asked. "Isn't it a little late for that? I mean, with a CEO looking at federal racketeering charges?"

Max had been struggling to keep a swirl of linguine from sliding off his fork, and giving up, he reached for his wine instead. Across the desk, the Beak was visibly amused. Max noticed and glared.

"It's not your skills at the table that cause me to smile," the Beak said. "It's your question. We have always considered our business legitimate, to adopt your term. We are a provider of goods and services that are in great demand but are not otherwise available under our restrictive laws. That, my friend, will not change."

"So what's so new and different?" Max asked. "A succession tree—did I get that right?—isn't exactly a revolution."

"No, not in and of itself, but it is part of what my son calls a paradigm shift—a top-to-bottom rethinking of how we do business. He said I had let myself get too bogged down in the details of our scattered enterprises—how much this bookmaker was producing or whether that shylock was kicking up a proper share of his earnings. He said getting mired in the minutiae was like trying to boil the ocean, when what was really called for was a thirty-thousand-foot view of the business as a whole."

Max felt his eyes glazing over. "Huh?" he said. "You're losing me."

"I sympathize, Detective," the Beak replied. "This MBA lingua franca is as foreign to me as it no doubt is to you. It was not among the languages offered at the University of Palermo, where my father sent me for the coat of veneer I still wear at age fifty-four. I confess I am not yet fully fluent. Perhaps a *digestivo* would help us both."

Max nodded. The Beak flashed a thumb and forefinger at the flunky and said, "*Due limoncelli, per favore.*"

The drinks appeared. It was sweet for Max's taste, but it was alcohol, and he downed it gratefully. The Beak signaled for a refill, and Max gulped that too.

"So you quit boiling the ocean," he said, setting down his glass, "and soared to thirty thousand feet—have I got that much right so far?"

"You have the metaphors right at least," the Beak said. "Truly understanding them, as I discovered, is quite another thing. I am the don, but I found myself deferring to Luca as the prophet, and he proposed doing what prophets historically have done, among them our Lord and Savior: a retreat to the desert to sort things out."

"Mafiosi in the burning sands? Hard to picture."

The Beak laughed. "Touché, Detective. What we saw of the burning sands was through the tinted windows of a Mercedes limousine, and our retreat was actually a resort hotel in Rancho Mirage, California. Appropriate, wouldn't you say, if the purpose of our meditations was not easing the plight of the poor but defending the sanctity of wealth—specifically, our own?"

"Rancho Mirage sounds like an appropriate name for planning your future," Max said drily. "RICO was still gonna be there when you got back to reality."

"As we both understood, Detective—that was the point of the pilgrimage. In Luca's view—"

"From thirty thousand feet?"

"In fact, yes, I suppose, if one accepts his adopted metaphor. His view is that we have too many scattered enterprises, which maximize our exposure to that dreadful law and don't earn enough to make them worth the risk. Luca's strong recommendation was that we—what was his word?—that we sunset most of them and concentrate on what he called our core competency: what we do best and what maximizes our earnings. 'Focus on our deliverables' is the way he put it. 'Stick to the products and services we can market at the least risk for the largest reward.'"

"Let me guess," Max said. "Drugs?"

"You said that, not I," the Beak answered.

"We're still off the record here. I have every reason to wish you life in supermax without parole, which, to me, would be a fate worse than death. But I agreed up front that what we discuss in these negotiations stays between us, and I honor my agreements."

"As do I, Detective. So long as you honor our core agreement, you will have your son back, and we can go our separate ways. But since circumstance has brought us together, I feel comfortable being candid with you—up to a point, naturally. I'm as proud of my son as you are of yours. We have that in common, do we not?"

"It's about all we have in common, I'd say, and there's a big difference even there. My son is a prisoner, a hostage. Yours is free to coin money with his hedge fund and design a RICO-repellent future for the mob. Too late to save his father, sadly."

"Sadly, yes, unless I can find a way to dissuade Mr. Trubble from bearing false witness against me."

"Or clip him before your case gets to court?"

The Beak, in his beam of light, looked sharply at Max in the surrounding darkness. "I would much prefer reasoning with him," he said, "but thus far, we don't even know where he is."

"Which puts us in the same fix," Max said, "since I don't know where Jay is. It limits one's options, doesn't it?"

"My compliments on your sense of irony, Detective—it is the true mark of a serious man. We are both seekers without compasses to guide us to our goals." The Beak signaled the flunky in the corner. "Should we have a different *digestivo*— something a little stronger to ease the suspense we both feel?"

Max nodded. The Beak flicked a forefinger. "*Due* Fernet-Branca, *favore*," he said, and in barely a minute, the drinks arrived. The taste was bitter to Max's tongue, but he raised his glass to the Beak and faked an appreciative smile to keep the conversation going.

"For me," the Beak said, "I suppose the ultimate irony is that I had paid for Trubble's defense when there was still a chance for him to survive."

"How so?"

"He panicked at the indictment purporting to link us as parties to a purported criminal conspiracy. I tried to calm him. I had my lawyers recruit a highly capable defense team for him. When he protested that he couldn't afford the cost, I offered him considerably more than a distress-sale price for some of his properties."

"Which properties?" Max asked. "The clubs? The real-estate holdings?"

The Beak smiled. "Would you leave me with no trade secrets, my friend?" he asked. "My point is, my lawyers and his—lawyers I paid for—would have given us at least a chance at surviving this frame-up. Instead, his team negotiated a trade: his testimony in exchange for his freedom and a new life in West Outer Nowhere."

"And you felt you'd insured yourself against that virus?"

"No insurance is absolute," the Beak said, polishing off his Fernet-Branca and signaling for another round. "But Luca is quite fierce on the question of security risks and has proposed changes to tighten the bolts, so to speak. We will, for example, no longer rely on outsiders like the Reverend Mr. Trubble for our retail operations—those jobs will be handled solely by men of honor. Made men, in the vernacular. Stand-up men. Men who have taken the oath of silence we call omertà."

Max stifled a laugh. "And that's your tightened security? You're a pretty trusting soul. Look how well the vow of omertà has served the other dons. I mean, when you've got soldiers, capos, underbosses, and even a boss singing like the fat lady in the opera, it looks to me like the game is about over."

The Beak considered his drink for a moment, ultimately leaving it untouched. "I am far from trusting, Detective," he said. "You yourself spoke of my success at rat-proofing the Paolucci borgata. It's partly because of measures I instituted when RICO was still a wet dream dampening some senator's sleep."

"Measures?"

"Measures. You doubtless have at least secondhand knowledge of our traditional initiation rites. The oath of allegiance sealed with drops of blood from a pinprick or a nick with a knife?"

Max nodded.

"It struck me that a pinprick was not an adequate deterrent to treason."

"So?"

"I substituted the slow extraction of a fingernail. Not, of course, on the trigger finger or even on the gun hand—those would be impediments to work. I usually chose the pinkie or the ring finger on the off hand and proceeded slowly, so as to prolong the pain and drive home the message."

"The message being?"

"This is only a taste of the pain you'll experience if you betray your don and your new family. The penalty is no longer a merciful two behind the left ear. It is two weeks—two weeks minimum—of pain so excruciating the miscreant will beg for death."

"Which sets an example for others tempted to betray you?"

"Precisely. What makes pain so useful as a management tool is its multiplier effect. It is a fact of human nature that we do not suffer pain in silence. When we experience it, we tell our friends about it, hoping, I suppose, to elicit their sympathy. In fact, we are bearing a message: 'Look out. This could happen to you.'"

"And it's you who inflicts the pain? The personal touch?"

"Of course," the Beak said, smiling. "I am not a library student of pain. I conduct my own original research."

"But what if the feds disappear potential snitches into witness protection before you can, ah, pursue your studies on them?"

"A fair question, Detective. In the time of RICO, two people merely seen in a room together can open themselves to a charge of conspiracy, which is why my son counseled a radical restructuring of our organization. Starting, I might add, with cutting down the number of rooms even remotely likely to come under federal surveillance. We shut down our social club in East Harlem, and we gave up our regular table at our favorite *ristorante*, Rao's."

"Where tables are hard to come by—I've never been able to crack the code. Is it as good as its word of mouth?"

"Better," the Beak said, reprising his wistful smile. "But as Luca reminded me, sacrifice is required in any radical reform. He persuaded me that we needed to right-size both our range of enterprises and our workforce."

"Which usually means downsizing," Max said. "I know that much of the lingo."

"Sadly, yes. I had to let some of our longest-tenured people go, men who had served our borgata since my father's day. It was a most difficult time and a difficult task for me." The Beak's eyes were suddenly misty. "I had my human resources department handle it."

"Wait—you have a fucking human resources department? In a Cosa Nostra family?"

"At Luca's strong urging, yes. He said, 'You're bringing bad news to men who've lived by the gun, the blade, and the garrote all their lives. You don't want to do that face-to-face.'"

"And you didn't?"

"I didn't, and I feel bad about it. Evidently, I haven't yet wholly adjusted to modernity—to the world Luca has been building around me. It is a world without sentiment, I'm afraid. My son was quite displeased when I doubled the size of the severance packages he'd proposed. The men we've RIF'd are wealthier in retirement than they were on the street, and if they wish to continue their businesses on their own, they may, with the understanding that we can no longer protect them—they're strictly on their own."

"And—I'm guessing here—the further understanding of what awaits them if they rat out their former employers?"

"Naturally," the Beak said. "Would a prudent man cut them adrift without that assurance?"

"I suppose not. And if I understood you earlier, you're closing out some of the traditional family businesses?"

"All of them but one, Detective. During our retreat, Luca and I did a meticulous risk-reward evaluation of each of our traditional enterprises. It was something I should have done long before, but those enterprises and the men who ran them were my inheritance, my legacy from my father. I accepted them as the way things were."

"Let me guess," Max said. "Your son felt no such sentiment for the past."

"You've guessed correctly," the Beak said. "Luca has been of the life but has observed it largely from a distance. He is a new man without a past to romanticize."

"And no regrets at severing his family from its past? I thought you said you were the ruthless one."

"As I am, in defense of my family. Luca's morality is founded not in sentiment but in numbers. In his view, we live in what he calls a binary world. Good and bad are not theological principles for him. Good and bad are what he calls measurables, and Judgment Day awaits not at God's throne but at the bottom line."

"And you're okay with that?"

"I am okay with anything that ensures the survival and prosperity of the Paolucci borgata, and if that means cutting our ties to our past, so be it."

"No more shylocking? No more gambling? No more hijacking? No more garbage hauling at extortionate prices? No more corrupting unions?"

"You can stop there, Detective—the answer is none of the above. Gambling has been socialized by the state or licensed to the Indians, and the others you've mentioned are open invitations to RICO prosecutions. Your federal colleagues have wires everywhere and more informers than they can house under new names in new places. We've become quite risk averse in the new paradigm."

"So you're bidding tradition goodbye."

"A tradition born centuries ago in the hills and villages of Sicily. But it lives on in my heart and my son's, for all what he

71

calls his next-gen way of thinking. He is quite persuasive in his argument that we have a go-to market, one more lucrative by a factor of millions than all our other enterprises combined, and that it should be the sole focus of our family business."

"Let me guess again," Max said. "Your go-to market is drug trafficking."

"And let me repeat, Detective: you said that, not I. But purely hypothetically, let's suppose you're right, and let's apply a risk-reward measure to such an undertaking. The rewards would be enormous and the risks minimal, even in the age of RICO. Your so-called war on drugs is in its fifth decade, and where is the victory? The market keeps growing, the product line keeps multiplying, and the costs are vastly higher for the hunters than the hunted. No, my friend, your war isn't a war at all—it more nearly resembles a clown show."

A long silence fell between the two men, with Max, in the shadows, contemplating his options and the don, in his circle of light, waiting for a response that didn't come.

"You've barely touched your *digestivo*," the Beak said when the absence of words got awkward. "May I offer you something more to your taste?"

"No, I'm good," Max said. "But look—we've been sitting here for a couple of hours, two men from separate worlds with one thing in common. We're both dads. You're proud of your son; I'm proud of mine."

"All true," the Beak replied. "So far."

"As you said at the beginning, you hold all the cards."

"Also true."

"But let me offer a proposition. What if my wife and I paid the balance of your asking price right now, which I believe comes to fifteen million? Would you consider releasing Jay to us then?"

"I've considered that, and I reconsidered it again today, during what I thought was a good conversation. Good, that is, given our conflicting interests."

"And?"

"At the risk of seeming a man without feeling, I must tell

you that the answer, sadly, is no. The payment schedule we've agreed to remains in force."

"But why?" Max asked.

"The numbers," the Beak said. "Luca's pole star. His guiding light."

"What, your son said no? The prince overruled the king?"

"As I've said, he is a most persuasive young man. I've been reinvesting your payments in his hedge fund, at considerable profit to both of us. In his view, to move such a large sum of money in a single transaction would draw the attention of the government. As I live in the age of RICO, he lives in the shadow of Dodd-Frank and the regulatory state."

"And you submitted?" Max said. "The father bending to the son's will?"

"Only after extensive discussion. I asked him at one point to suppose the roles were reversed. Suppose he were your prisoner, and I was desperate to free him, would not blood matter more than business?"

"And he said?"

"He said, 'Pop, I hate to say it, but you must be getting old. The roles aren't reversed. You're being sentimental, and sentimentality has no place in business.'"

"And?"

"I had finally to admit he was right. Business is business always."

Max stared at the Beak through narrowed eyes. "Motherfucker," he said. "The man behind the curtain turns out to be a yellow-bellied, jive-time motherfucker."

The Beak returned his gaze with a wan half smile. "It's sad to end what has been an adult conversation on so childish a note. I suppose it's time to have my men take you home."

"I suppose so," Max said. "Thank you for your hospitality. I now know who I'm dealing with."

CHAPTER 8

He Has to Kill Me

"Sorry we lost you yesterday, boss," Ahab said. "I'll say this for Brother Beak: he's got himself one hell of a wheelman. Squaring blocks, fast turns, running lights, switching cars—those mob guys call that cleaning, from what I've heard, and that boy cleaned us good."

"Yeah," Max said. "We switched cars once too. After they knew they'd shaken you, from what I could overhear, but they clearly weren't taking any chances."

The two men were sitting in the upstairs living room, with Max in his preferred corner of the couch and Ahab in an earth-toned easy chair. The shade of Albert Camus was sitting silently and weightlessly on Ahab's lap, but Ahab seemed unaware of his presence; as a ghost practitioner, Camus was visible and palpable only to his clients.

"The Beak's got a smart-ass security guy too—that nerdy blond hippie from across the street. Look what he did to Mullarkey's magic glasses."

Max handed them across the coffee table to Ahab. They'd been snapped in two, and the mic had been extracted from its cache in the bridge. "So much for specs being search-proof," Max said. "My days as Mr. Peepers appear to be over."

"So'd you get any idea of where they took you?"

"They had me hooded going and coming, so all I know for sure is that we never left Manhattan—I'd have known from the sound if we'd taken a bridge or a tunnel. Beyond that, I'm guessing, but I'm pretty sure I was in Harlem."

"Feel of the street?" Ahab asked.

"Exactly," Max said. "You and I are grads of the same prep school: narco undercover working out of the Two-Six house. Schooling like that, Helen Keller would've known she was amongst the brothers."

"But no sense where in Harlem?"

"I'm guessing one of your white-whale friend Reverend Trubble's old venues. The Beak told me he bought up a bunch of them to help the rev pay for his RICO defense and keep him in line." Max laughed. "Didn't quite work out for him, though. Seems the feds flipped the rev and put him in the program. They've got him on ice somewhere until they need him to put Charles Beak in the slammer."

"But we don't know which venue?" Ahab asked.

"No. I figured I could talk to our old friend Satin about that—he knows all the happenings in Harlem, from the bottom side up and the top side down. But in a way, it doesn't matter, 'cause it's not where they're holding Jay. He's somewhere else."

"You were a long time with Brother Beak. Did you pick up any actionable intel?"

"Not really, no. I got a lot about how he and his son are turning the Paolucci family into General Motors, which I'll pass along to Tina for her Bureau boyfriend when this is over. I get you a day-old coffee, partner? I've got it heating up."

"Thanks, no, boss. I'm good."

"Wise choice. Dew makes it a lot better than I do." He got up to pour himself a cup, added a splash of rum, and carried it back to the couch. "Y'know, though," he said, "there's one thing I did come away with."

"Which is?"

"Which is that we've gotta figure out an action plan forthwith to spring Jay before the last payment moves eight days from today."

"Not easy, boss, when we don't know where our target is."

"I know," Max said.

"I take it you don't trust your new best friend to keep his end of the bargain?"

"No, I don't. It's purely instinct, but it tells me the Beak has no intention of letting Jay go—or me either. He talks a lot about filial love, but I think he plans to kill us both. Which means I've got to kill him first."

"I ain't tryin' to hear that killin' shit, son," Camus said when he and Max were alone. "You finna cook me up a pastis or what?"

Camus had spent a single evening in Harlem sixty years earlier, but in his postmortem visits with Max, he always affected the argot of the black street. He did so, he said, in deference to Max's shaky command of French, but he'd never otherwise explained his odd choice of a common tongue.

Max stirred up a pastis for his guest, added a second splash of Mount Gay to his cooling espresso, and set them down on the coffee table. "So," he said, "you're here to hassle me for wanting to kill the guy who snatched my son and is looking to kill him and me. I get that right?"

"You know I got much love for you, cuz, always, but sometime y'all mind wander way out there where the buses don't stop. I have to remind you they's a different between what you know and what you think you know? You finna smoke somebody, you best know for sure they out to smoke you."

"What I think I know is based on instinct, and when you're a cop as long as I was, your instincts get pretty fine-tuned. And would you mind using that coaster when you set down your drink? Dew will have my ass if she comes home and sees rings on that table. It's an Eames. It cost us beaucoup."

"*Désolé, mon vieux,*" Camus said, bending forward to wipe away the wet circles, imperfectly, with the elbow of his greatcoat. When he'd finished, he picked up his pastis, took a swallow, and set it down, again missing the coaster.

"Al," Max said. "For Christ's sake."

"Jus' schoolin' you about pain, B. We all cause it, an' it don't make no nevermind whether we mean to or not. You alive, you gonna hurt somebody."

"But most of us don't inflict pain for our own pleasure," Max said.

"Yeah, we do," Camus said. "You ain't never cheated on your wife?"

"Fuck you, Al. Like you didn't cheat on Francine."

"Yeah, but I tol' her. It hurt her, but it hurt me tellin' her. At least I paid my dues."

"But this guy Charlie Beak calls himself a student of pain. He likes hurting people, and right now, that's my son and me. If you don't believe me, you should have been at my lunch with him yesterday. He doesn't need to get physical to inflict pain."

"Didn't need to be there. Up in Ghost Town, where I stay, over near the sky, they was streamin' it in real time on I See Live People TV."

"Yeah, yeah," Max said. "You've told me I'm a TV star up there."

"So I'm kickin' it at the Last Stop Lounge with some of my boys: Dante, Melville, Eliot—"

"T. S. Eliot?"

"Naw, he a stiff. I'm talkin' 'bout George Eliot. She actually a lady, truth be known, but she had to be a pretend dude to get her shit published, and she like hangin' with us. So anyway, we sittin' up in there, knockin' back forties, when *The Max Show* come on that big ectoplasma flat-screen they got behind the bar."

"So I'm still a fuckin' show to you guys?"

"We ghosts, man. We got some pride. What you think we gonna watch—all this zombie shit y'all puttin' on TV down here? We wouldn't be watchin' that mess even if we had cable, which we don't. Them zombie shows givin' dead people a bad name. For real."

"My apologies on behalf of the living," Max said. "But if you watched that lunch, you saw what was going on. The guy was gaming me, letting me believe there was some wisp of a connection between us, dad to dad—like hey, maybe we can do a deal right here right now for my son's freedom. And you know what he was doing behind all that dad talk, all that sunny *mezzogiorno* hospitality, all that insiders' tour of the next-generation Mafia? He was torturing me. Tantalizing me into a box, a little-ease of the mind, and slamming it shut behind me."

"And you talkin' 'bout killing him behind that?" Camus said. "'Cause that mean man played wid your mind for a couple hours? You trippin', son."

"All respect, Al, but I don't think so. You want to know my takeaway from that meeting? He's setting me up. He'll wait till the last payday, at which point he'll propose a meet at some out-of-the-way place where he'll supposedly hand Jay over to me. Only he won't. He probably won't even be there—he'll be off lunching with some reliable alibi witnesses while his hitters kill me and Jay both and lose our bodies in some landfill somewhere."

"Why he do that? He got his twenty-fi' mil. That's some serious cake, B."

"'Cause he knows I can put a kidnapping case on top of his RICO problems. He knows I was a cop, and he knows cops don't let shit go. I've got our bank records; I've got him on a video with my son in chains. A kidnapping beef is a minimum fifteen to twenty-five in New York State, and I don't think Clarence Darrow and Johnny Cochran combined could get him out of that jam. He has to kill me. Jay too. Probably Meridew. Maybe Ahab—anybody he thinks knows anything."

"Unless you kill him first?"

"Unless I kill him first."

"And his son ain't gonna put a green light on your ass and send all them hitters after you? And your whole family? You gots to be out your mind."

"I guess I'll have to take my chances."

"Widout me, B. I don't book no killing, 'specially not if it come out what somebody *think* gonna happen. I'm more like my man Doc Rieux in *The Plague*. I ain't never got used to seein' people die."

"And what if it's me who dies, trying to free my son?"

"Guess I'll see it on TV back in Ghost Town," Camus said, already beginning to dissolve into a cloud of pixels. "Ain't no way I can he'p you, way you thinkin' right now. Peace out."

The BlackBerry in Max's breast pocket was vibrating. Max, lost in regret, thought of ignoring it, but when it buzzed a second time and a third, he clicked it on.

"Yo," he said.

"Yo back atcha, Dance," Tina said. "We need to talk."

"When?"

"How's right now?"

"Usual place?"

"I'm already there, and I don't have all day—I'm stealing time from a police-involved shooting, so get your ass over here."

"Please tell me it was a clean shoot," Max said.

"I wish," Tina said. "You know I'm always gonna cut some slack for a brother cop—he wants to get home alive at the end of tour same as anybody else. But this one? Eleven-year-old black kid comes out of the subway in Union Square with a plastic pirate sword—a fucking toy, Dance—and this knucklehead puts three in him. Nicks a couple bystanders besides. And of course, the officer's white. And there's at least five smartphone videos—I mean, you know what Union Square's like on a spring day with the green market open and all."

"The officer's a rookie? At least tell me that."

"Nah, guy's got seven years in. More than enough to know better, especially now."

Max sighed. "Especially now," he echoed. "Too many people already out here thinking cops got nothing to do but go out hunting young brothers."

"Tell me about it," Tina said. "Time I left the scene, there were already Black Lives Matter people handing out leaflets for the next protest march. I mean, as if our morale wasn't already in the shitter."

"So let me guess: you hand the case off to Internal Affairs."

"I still gotta write what I got, Dance. Every cop's favorite pastime—you remember that, right?"

"You hand the case off to IA, and you skip to Posto? You got something that important for me?"

"Yes and no. See you when I see you."

Ahab was standing at the foot of the stairs as Max descended. "You headed out, boss?" he asked.

"Yeah. Gotta see our girl about a thing."

"You need me to run interference? That goombah from across the street's got the corner staked out again. I can disorient him if you want."

"Aw, fuck him," Max said. He winked at Ahab and, with a toss of his head, indicated the stairway. Ahab winked back as Max started up toward his backdoor route to freedom.

It started with a climb up the fire escape to the roof of his town house, past the top-floor apartment he rented cheap to a couple of overworked, underpaid residents from the Hospital for Joint Diseases across Second Avenue. If they noticed his passage to the roof at all, he guessed they probably diagnosed it as further evidence that he was a nutjob—who else would lease a nicely furnished two-bedroom in Manhattan at flophouse prices? His path from there led over twelve intervening rooftops and down another fire escape into the patch of garden behind the last brownstone on the block. The ground floor there was occupied by three aged-out flower children who were typically stoned on weed or zoned on Zen; either way, they'd wave him through their pad and wish him peace as he stepped outside at the far end of the block.

He found Tina sipping a diet cola at their usual booth at Posto. A tumbler of barbera appeared on their table without his having to ask. There were benefits to being a regular at a New York restaurant, and one of them at Posto was knowing Jess, a part-time server whose real gift was stand-up comedy; her day job helped pay her bills and sustain her dream.

Her further talent was discretion. She knew that when she saw Max and Tina together, it was all business; she plunked

Max's glass on the table and retreated to her station near the till at the end of the bar.

"So what have you got for me, T?" Max asked, settling in. "Anything on where my son might be at?"

"Not a lot, and some of it's pretty vague. Both my Bureau guy and my girl at OCCB are pretty sure his primary residence is some kind of spread up in Westchester, but they can't pinpoint where. There's nothing in his name, obviously."

"Or Auntie Agnese's?" Max asked. "Her name's on more stuff than Donald Trump's. If that lady knew everything she supposedly owns, she wouldn't be living in that bungalow in Island Park."

"If she ever knew, which I doubt, she forgot," Tina said. "My intel is she's got stage-three Alzheimer's. But there's nothing in her name up there. Zero. Zilch. Nada."

"And that's probably where he's got Jay. My guess anyway."

"Mine too, Dance. If we only knew where it is. I told my boy Digger you'd probably pay him some green to spend a day or two up there seeing what he could find in the county clerk's office—that's where they keep all the deeds. Was I out of line?"

"Fuck no, girl. Tell him I'll pay him my day rates and double it if he scores."

"He wasn't real optimistic, Dance."

Max laughed. "Was he ever?" he said. "What else you got?"

"Okay, we know Beaky's got three apartments in Manhattan and two in Brooklyn. The only one he uses on any kind of regular basis is in that new glass condo tower over by First Avenue, in the lower Sixties. The skinny one with the affordable housing for a few token peasants? I've got the exact address in my desk, but you know the one I'm talking about. We think the others are all either trap houses or safe houses—pick 'em."

Max ordered another barbera. "So tell me about his place in the tower," he said. "What do we know?"

"He bought a duplex penthouse and sectioned off the downstairs as a bunkhouse for his security guys—six soldiers, plus two techies who sweep the place twice a day for taps and bugs. They live there, but the Beak only stays over if he's

81

got business in town. He's a commuter, like half the people working in the city." She sipped her Coke. "Hey, can a girl get a slice around here?"

Max made a triangle with his thumbs and forefingers and mouthed, "Two." Two slices of pizza soon appeared.

"And?" Max asked. "Anything else?"

"One other thing—Digger says our boy Charlie B bought up a whole bunch of the Rev Trubble's properties in Harlem and Bed-Stuy, including that so-called church the rev was using for his main stash. All in the name of Agnese Properties, a member corporation of Agnese Worldwide Enterprises."

"Yeah, I know about the shopping spree," Max said, mimicking a smug smile. "The Beak told me about those deals over lunch yesterday."

"He what? Pardon my Sicilian, but you had lunch with fucking Charlie fucking Beak? The man who kidnapped your son?"

"Yeah, I did. I'm not sure where, 'cause his boys had a hood over my head going and coming, but my best guess, we were in that church, in Trubble's old pastoral office. The place had that smell about it."

"The sweet smell of yayo," Tina said. "So Beaky told you about buying up Trubble World?"

"Yeah. Kind of a fire-sale deal—the rev needed money lawyering up for his RICO trial, and the Beak figured he could buy his loyalty by buying his real estate. Didn't quite work out for him, though."

"I know. My boy at the Bureau told me they flipped the rev. Got him on ice somewhere in Arizona or Kansas—one of those places. They all look the same to a Jersey girl like me. They sneak him back to town when they need him." She took a bite of pizza, chewing it contemplatively. "So'd you get anything you can use to get Jay back?"

"Not a damn thing, really. What I got was a lot of sentimental fathers-and-sons talk—how proud we are of our boys. The only difference being he's holding my boy hostage while he's grooming his as his successor. I also got a lot about their plans for revolutionizing how they do business, which I'll give you a full debrief on when this is over. Get you some brownie points with the OCCB and the Bureau."

"Why not now, Dance?"

"Can't risk it till I get Jay back. I'll tell you then. Promise."

A quiet minute passed with the two old partners feigning interest in their pizza.

"So that's it?" Max said, breaking the silence. "You sounded pretty urgent on the phone."

"Yeah, well, this next is a little hard for me. This off-the-record rule works both ways, right?"

"We rode together eight years, and you're gonna ask if we can trust each other? T, please."

"Yeah, well, you remember once long ago I mentioned I had a great-uncle who was a made man in the Anastasia crime family?"

"Yeah, vaguely. So?"

"It's stuff I don't normally talk about—I mean, I got a career on the line here, so I don't like calling attention to that branch of my family."

"Look, T, your great-uncle was a wiseguy; my parents were Commies. What difference does it make? We're not them; we're us."

"I guess. The bosses haven't shit-canned me yet, so I guess they're not gonna."

"Not with the number of wiseguys you've cuffed," Max said. "So talk, girl."

"It's just there's a guy from that part of the family I think could help you out," Tina said. "An uncle of mine. His name's Nicola Malatesta, but he goes by his work name, Nick Testa. He does what you do—he's got PI licenses in six or seven states, last I heard. He just does it—" She paused.

"Does it what?" Max said. "Spit it out, T."

"He does it differently—put it that way," she replied. "Real tough guy. Special Forces in Iraq—both wars—plus Afghanistan. They're not trained to be nice."

"Which branch? I'm just curious."

"He doesn't like to talk about it much. Did what he calls some government work after that, which he doesn't say much about either. He did mention an extraction over in the South Sudan but never said who they extracted from what kind of jam. That was what made me think he could help get Jay home."

"Interesting. A tough kid in that wing of the family and never got mobbed up? How's that happen?"

"I don't know, Dance—I guess he was too much of a loner. They wanted him, but he skipped and joined the military instead. I think I was the only member of the whole clan he ever really felt close to. He used to babysit me when he was in high school and I was little. Still calls me every couple or three months to see how I'm doing. I ask him how he's doing, and he says, 'Fine,' and clams up."

"So how's bringing in another PI help my situation?"

Tina paused again, brushing a crumb of pizza crust from the sleeve of her blazer. "He's not just another PI," she said. "He's what you might call a specialist. He calls himself a closer, and where you're at right now, your situation, a closer might be just what you need."

This time, it was Max who paused, doing his own risk-reward assessment.

"Y'know, T," he said finally, "normally, the cop in me would say thanks but no thanks; I can handle this myself. But there's nothing normal about the jam I'm in right now. How do I reach the guy?"

"You don't," Tina said. "Nick lives under the radar. I gave him your digits. He'll contact you."

CHAPTER 9

The Pleasure of Pain

"So Tina says this mystery man of hers will get in touch with me in a couple of days," Max said. He'd gotten home and found Meridew unpacking. "We haven't got a couple of days, babe. We've only got five banking days left, plus the weekend. According to my math, that gives us seven days total to get Jay back, and that's assuming Mr. Beak keeps his word."

"The desperate hours," Meridew said, snuggling closer to Max on the couch. "I'm almost sorry Edith and I managed to get the bank straightened out on keeping to the schedule we gave them. I swear I felt as if I were speaking Kiswahili to some of those suits. You'd think it was their money."

"I thought Henry's father was seeing to all that himself. No, huh?"

"He did his best, love, really, but I'm afraid he's lost a step."

"Really? He's not that old."

"No, he isn't. But I think the scandal Henry brought down on the family took a lot out of him. I mean, what was the *Post* headline? 'Mogul Slain in Love Nest' or something like that? Philadelphia society, shall we say, did not approve."

Max threw an arm around Meridew's shoulders, pulled

her tight, and kissed her. "Damn, Dew," he said, "I'm glad you're home."

"You missed me?" she asked.

"You're kidding, right?" he said. "I mean, leave out my long-term hopes for us—you've heard all that before. It's just we're in a crisis now, and you bring the calm at the eye of the storm. You're the one person I can talk to. I can't tell Tina everything. I can't tell Ahab everything."

"What about Camus?" she asked, suppressing a smile. Max had told her long before about his conversations with his visitor from Ghost Town, and she'd done him the kindness of accepting them as part of his reality, if not her own or anyone else's.

"Camus?" he said. "He fired me."

"Fired you?" she said. "Why?"

"Because I want to kill this sadist motherfucker who's stolen our son, that's why. He doesn't approve."

"I accept your belief in ghosts, love, but I think that may be your conscience talking. I know there are things you've had to do, but I still know you better than anyone, and killing isn't in your nature."

"Maybe, maybe not. We'll see."

"You know, love," she said, breaking a silence, "sometimes I think you don't tell *me* everything."

"I do, babe," he said. "I've maybe blurred some things I think might cause you pain, but—"

"You're not understanding me, Max. This is our pain, not yours to carry alone because you're the man in the family. I need to know all of it. Everything."

"But—"

"No buts allowed here, love. You're blurring details because I'm a woman, and you think that makes me—I don't know—a fragile flower. You've lived in a man's world too long. Women are stronger than you think. I'm stronger than you think."

"I know that, Dew, but—"

"For instance, I took care of the problem of Jay missing classes and basketball practices. I knew you wouldn't—as Jay said, you're not that good at making stuff up."

86

"You put in the fix?" Max asked. "How'd you manage that?"

"I told them I'd called a two-week family retreat because I was considering entering politics and wanted my husband and my son to be part of my decision."

"And they bought that?" Max said, chuckling. "Please."

"They bought it partly because I also pledged a couple million to their building fund. But it's true, love. Prematurely true—I'm thinking way down the road, after Jay graduates—but still true."

"You're really?"

"I'm really. I'm sick of just volunteering one day a week at a ghetto school and writing checks to Planned Parenthood and Doctors without Borders. I want to—I don't know. I want to give my time, my energy—myself, really. I'm tired of being a cheerleader on the sidelines. I want to be in the game."

"But—"

"Jay was gung ho for the idea—I mean, before all this. He wants to be part of it, and he will be. I'll want your support too, love. I wouldn't do it without my husband's consent. I am, after all, only a girl."

Max slumped forward on the couch, his hands dangling between his knees. "I do have a gift, don't I?"

Meridew smiled. "You have many gifts, love," she said. "They're why I married you."

"I'm talking about my gift for underestimating my wife," he said. "Should I fix us a drink?"

"That would be nice," she said. "And let's order out for dinner. I don't feel much like cooking, and my guess is you don't either. Agreed?"

"Agreed," Max said.

Max was measuring out a kir for Meridew, when the New New Girl buzzed. "That guy Don whatever is on line two for you. I told him you're busy, like you said, but he says you'll want to pick up. Sorry, boss."

"You did right, kid," Max said. "Put him through."

"*Buona sera,* Signore Christian," the Beak's voice said. "We have an issue we need to discuss."

"An issue besides your snatching my son?" Max asked.

"Let's say it's a closely related issue, one that will affect him as well as you."

"Hold on a sec while I put you on speaker," Max said. "My wife is back home, and she'll want to hear this."

"As you wish, Detective. In my world, we spare our women the sometimes unpleasant details of our lives as a matter of respect for their sensibilities. If you wish your wife to be exposed to what I'm about to tell you, that is your choice. And hers, I suppose."

"Her choice is to be spared no details, no matter how unpleasant. She is Jay's parent too." Max glanced at Meridew. She nodded. He jabbed the speaker button. "You're on the air, motherfucker. What's on your ugly mind?"

"It has come to my attention," the Beak said, "that a certain gentleman spent a day and a half in the Westchester County clerk's offices, going through files and asking questions about property holdings in my name and the names of certain enterprises associated with me."

"You found out? What, a little birdie told you? You heard it through the grapevine?"

"Let's just say I have friends in many places high and low, and one of them is a supervisor in the clerk's office. She alerted us to the presence of this gentleman and, I might add, his persistence. So I sent two of my employees there yesterday to see if they could be of assistance."

"Yeah, right," Max said. "The Paolucci travelers'-aid service. Part of your new business model no doubt. So what's this got to do with me?"

"Please, Detective, don't try my patience. This person told my men at first that he was doing academic research on the distribution of wealth in the New York exurbs. But with a little prompting, he identified himself as a retired detective second grade: Richard Calhoun, known also as Digger for his prowess at exploring public records."

"Yeah, so? I knew the guy way back in the day, but I

retired from the NYPD eight years ago. I lost touch with him. It happens."

"Interesting, Detective," the Beak said. "Because with further prompting, Mr. Calhoun told my men he was in your employ, in connection with a case you were working on."

"I hate to think what kind of prompting your boys used," Max said.

"Mild prompting, Detective, I can assure you. Your Mr. Calhoun did not exactly qualify as a profile in courage. And happily for you, I might add, he had no knowledge of why you wanted the information he was seeking or what use you planned to make of it. At least you've adhered to that part of our initial agreement—you haven't shared your situation with the police."

"If your boys hurt that old man, I'll—"

"You'll what, Detective? Need I remind you yet again of your powerlessness?"

"Fuck you," Max said. He felt Meridew's glare of reproof without looking.

"Your vulgarisms are themselves an admission that you have no viable options," the Beak said. "As it happens, Mr. Calhoun's acquaintance with my boys, as you call them, had a modestly rough beginning, but they parted on amicable terms. My men, as I call them, offered him a ride home to the city and waved goodbye to him at the door to his apartment building. If you doubt me, call him yourself. He'll tell you he sustained nothing worse than a bruise or two."

"I hope you're right. That's all I can say."

"You will, however, be disappointed by his findings—or, rather, his lack thereof. Given another day or two rummaging through deeds and transfers, he might have found something of interest to you, but my men persuaded him to give up his quest."

"So no harm done, right?"

"Wrong, Detective. The mere fact of this research project, so-called, suggests a serious breach of faith on your part—a prelude perhaps to attempting some sort of quixotic rescue mission. Someone must pay for this transgression, and since I have your son, it is he who will bear the punishment."

"But why?" Meridew blurted. Max could see at a glance that she was fighting back tears. "You've nullified any possible threat on our part. You've won. Why must you punish our son for something that hasn't happened and can't happen?"

"I understand your concern, signora," the Beak said. "As your husband has doubtless told you, I have a son of my own. But I'm afraid your question is best directed to Signore Christian, not to me. My reading of his history tells me he is an angry man and dangerous when his anger is aroused. One defeat will not end the threat such a man poses."

"Look," Max said, "what I'd like to do is one thing, and what I can do is something else. Like you said earlier, I'm out of options. You don't need a deterrent. I'm raising the white flag, and I'm begging you, father to father, please don't hurt my boy."

"I'm sorry, but my course is set. What must be done must be done. And besides, I have a new experiment I'm eager to run."

"You're going to experiment?" Meridew said. "On our son? A boy not yet out of his teens?"

"A limited experiment—a first step in a new line of research I'm opening. I am in many ways an old-fashioned man, but like everyone else, I am affected by the popular culture we all inhabit. You're doubtless aware of the vogue for all things organic—a quart of milk, a head of lettuce, a cut of meat, a jar of supplements?"

"Yeah," Max said. "So?"

"I plan to embark on a syllabus of organic pain, and your son is an ideal subject—young, strong, athletic, in fine physical condition. And, I might add, quite expressive. He does not conceal his feelings. Perfect for my needs."

"You're beginning to sound like Dr. Frankenstein here," Max said. "Exactly what sort of mad organic science do you propose to inflict on our son?"

"Exposure to the sting of the bullet ant, species *Paraponera clavata*," the Beak said. "Have you ever heard of it?"

"No," Max said. "I can't say I like the sound of it."

"As indeed you shouldn't. Its sting is said to cause the most excruciating pain known to man. It is native to Brazil, and the Sateré-Mawé people there use it in their initiation rites, welcoming a boy into manhood. They fashion a rudimentary pair of mitts out of leaves, fill them with bullet ants, and place the initiate's hands in them. The initiate is said to experience a level of pain beyond even my imagining, and I am hardly a beginning student. If he cannot endure it, he cannot be counted as a warrior or even a man."

"It sounds like something you'd cook up for *your* initiation rites. The making of a made man."

"Don't think the thought hasn't occurred to me, Detective. Extracting fingernails has been an effective check against betrayal, but the pain inflicted by the bullet ant is worse by an order of magnitude. I have a supply of a hundred of these interesting creatures, provided me by a business associate in South America. They are happily multiplying as we speak."

"Let me guess—your source is El Sandman?" Max asked. "The last of the great Colombian *narcotrafficantes*?"

"As I said, a business associate—his identity is of no importance here. Suffice it to say he knows of my studies and felt that these ants could take my research to a newer, higher level of pain. I can scarcely wait to test their potency."

"To test it on my son."

"On your son. I suppose you could say he is in the wrong place at the wrong time. But his experience with the bullet ant will be limited—I am, after all, not immune to paternal feeling, and with a few exceptions, he has been a well-behaved guest. An initiate among the Sateré-Mawé is required to wear the gloves on both hands for ten minutes of exquisite pain— pain that will only keep intensifying for the ensuing eight hours and last for as many as twenty-four. Your son will wear a glove on one hand for five minutes, half the time and exposure demanded of native boys younger than he. I am not entirely without compassion, Detective, no matter what you think of me."

"You sadistic motherfucker," Max said.

91

"I should remind you, Detective, *sadistic* is a compliment for me. It aptly describes my scholarly absorption with pain."

"Except your own."

"I am simply an observer, a scientist in his laboratory. My subjects are not rats or mice or frogs; they are human beings. Much of our understanding of pain is quite primitive—we are not far past the theories advanced by René Descartes more than three centuries ago, and yet we continue to base our studies on the behavior of laboratory animals instead of humans, for whom pain is a subjective as well as objective experience. Rodents cannot express what they feel. Humans can."

"And you enjoy observing them in pain?" Max asked. "Expressing it?"

"Yes, I confess that I do. And I must further confess that it is not the simple pleasure of the scientist advancing the sum of human knowledge. Human pain, for me, is an art form. It is a spectacle, an entertainment. It is stimulating to watch."

Max and Meridew exchanged "Oh my God" glances. Meridew could no longer hold back her tears. Max reached for her hand and squeezed it in his.

"And you propose to have fun inflicting pain on my son?" he asked.

"Oh, I will," the Beak said. "I'll email you a video if you like. I might even post it on YouTube if it's as satisfying as I expect it to be."

The BlackBerry lying next to Max's side of the bed started vibrating loudly at three thirty in the morning, when there was never good news. "Yo," he said, and then he added, "What the fuck?"

"It's Tina," the voice on the phone said. "What, I woke you up?"

"No, I was in my game room, playing *Grand Theft Auto*, or I woulda been if I fucking had a game room," Max said. "What do you think I was doing at three-whatever in the morning?"

"Dance, the shit jumped bad," Tina said. "They got Digger."

"They fucking what?"

"They iced Digger. He took both barrels of a shotty, double-O buck, in the chest and belly. Tore the poor guy wide open. I'm at his place looking at him right now."

"Give me five to get dressed; I'll be right there. Peter Cooper Village, right? My old 'hood? I've got his digits somewhere."

"Are you out of your fucking mind, Dance? In your situation, this is the last place on the planet you want to show your face."

"But the old guy was working for me, T. I knew they found out what he was up to, but from what they told me, they let him go with a couple bruises."

"What who told you? Your pal Charlie Beak?"

"Matter of fact, yeah. Said two of his hoods snatched him at the Westchester county clerk's office. Said it didn't take much rough stuff for Digger to give up what he was doing and who he was doing it for."

"That part I can believe," Tina said. "The old man had no street in him. Never did. All he ever chased was paper."

"Right. So according to the Beak, they drove him home and waved goodbye at the door—end of story. My guess is they're alibied for the hit."

"My guess too. My guess is Charlie handed this one off to his boy Il Lupo—which, by the way, is what Sicilian wiseguys call their shotguns. In fact, that's how Il Lupo got his nickname. From what my girl at OCCB tells me, that fat skel always favored a shotty for a piece of work."

"Damn, I belong there, T," Max said. "He was my guy, working my case."

"Forget it, Dance—you need to go back to your imaginary game room and finish that game. Digger was my guy too on a lot of cases. I'll represent your interests here. I caught the case, me and my boy Jamil."

"Your canvass turn up anything?"

"Not a whole lot so far. Everybody awake at the time heard the shotty—no way you can silence those fuckers—and we picked up two or three peephole peepers who saw the two guys leaving. Consensus was one of 'em was a seriously big guy, like the Hulk on 'roids—I'm guessing that was Il Lupo. The other guy—I dunno. Tall blond dude with a ponytail is all we're getting so far."

"Yeah, I think I know who Blondie is. I don't have a name, but he's one of the Beak's boys in the listening post I've told you about, across from my office. Plus, he was in the car that took me to lunch with the gentleman don himself. Il Lupo was the muscle, but Blondie seemed to be the one running the show. Which was weird 'cause he's not your standard-issue wiseguy. Coulda been a college buddy of the Beak's kid, if I had to guess."

"You pick up anything past guessing? A first name, maybe? Anything your girl can use?"

"No," Max said. "I could pick him out of a photo array, but that's about it. Those guys were too disciplined to call each other by name with an ex-cop aboard. Sorry, kid."

"That's okay for now, Dance," Tina said. "For now, we're playing this as a home-invasion robbery by persons unknown, which is exactly what your friends want us to think. They turned the place upside down and walked with everything looked like it was worth anything. They even got his life savings out of his sock drawer—you believe that? Poor old guy told me once he didn't believe in banks—not after what he'd seen in their financials. Only took two broken fingers to get him to give that up."

"Jesus. They get that antique computer of his too?"

"'Fraid so, Dance. We're fucked there."

"Yeah, T. If he had anything, it would've been in there. My guess is Blondie scrubbed the hard drive before they even got back to whatever cave they came from. You'll keep me posted?"

"You're even asking? I just didn't want you to be surprised if you see me quoted in the press as calling this a robbery-murder, plain and simple. It's too soon to call it mob related and let the Beak know we're on to him. I got your back, Dance."

"And I got yours, T," Max said. "Anything I get, you got—word. Now, get back to work before Chief Briscoe shows up and burns your ass for sexting on duty."

CHAPTER 10

The Closer

It was the sudden buzz of the BlackBerry in his jeans pocket that rescued Max from his third attempt at witnessing the torment of his son at the hands of the Student of Pain. The video of Jay and the bullet ants had arrived by email that morning. Max's partner was out chasing the purloined Porterfield diamonds, and his wife had excused herself from the viewing; her insistence on hearing everything did not require her to see everything, which condemned Max to watch Jay's agony alone.

He'd sat for a good while staring at the newcomer to his in-box, a message from a sender named painstudies@agneselab. edu with the subject line "P. clavata 1.01." A glance at his Timex had told Max it was 10:17 on the morning of May 2, four days from Jay's expiration date and, more than likely, his own. He'd poured himself a short shot of Mount Gay and downed it, hoping it would bring him courage; finding none, he'd followed up with a stronger pour to minimal effect. He'd checked his other emails; they were mostly spam from wine merchants and budget clothiers. He'd buzzed the New New Girl to see if there had been any calls; she'd told him a bit impatiently that there'd been none so far, but she'd be sure to let him know if any came in. He'd filled in a couple of the trickier entries in the *Times*'s Saturday crossword but had gotten stuck on a third and shoved the paper aside.

Finally, he'd clicked on the painstudies email and opened the video attachment. It started with a shot of Jay sitting bare-chested and alone on a stark white chair in a stark white room. From off camera, the Beak's unmistakable voice intoned, "The following is experiment one-point-oh-one exploring the levels of pain induced by the sting of ants of the species *Paraponera clavata*, known commonly as bullet ants, native to Brazil and Central America. A fellow scholar of pain studies has rated the intensity of the ant's sting at four-plus on a scale of one to four. To put that finding more colloquially, the pain was off the charts."

The camera zoomed in on Jay's face. His eyes were heavy-lidded, and his lower lip was slack and trembling. "Our subject," the Beak continued, "is a well-formed male college student athlete, age eighteen, who volunteered to participate in the study. He has been mildly sedated with liquid diazepam to reduce the possibility of anxiety exaggerating the level of pain actually felt. My laboratory assistant will now begin by inserting the subject's right hand into a common oven mitt containing twenty-five bullet ants, each roughly an inch long, all freshly aroused from a natural anesthesia. The subject's hand will remain in the mitt for precisely five minutes."

A bulky man in white scrubs and latex gloves materialized beside Jay, yanked him roughly to his feet, jammed his hand into the ant's nest, and held it there. Within seconds, Jay's eyes bugged wide. His face turned a violent red. His jaw dropped. His mouth was a rictus of pain. He screamed a long, piercing wail that had drained the last drop of Max's will and sent him scuttling across the hall just in time to vomit copiously into the bathroom sink.

On his second try, he'd endured the bugged eyes, the contorted mouth, the crimson face, and the shrieks of agony; he'd made it all the way to the point at which the time code showed 5:00:00, and the Beak's man freed Jay from the mitt. His hand was swollen and pewter gray. His face had gone from tomato red to a ghastly white. He screamed again and went careening around the room with his hands waving over his head and his legs pumping high, his body bouncing off walls, until he finally crumpled to the floor and curled up in a fetal ball.

"The pain will continue and intensify over the next eight hours," the Beak's voice was saying when Max once again reached the limits of his own capacity for pain. He'd hunched over his wastebasket and retched again, dry-heaving this time but unable to stop the retroperistaltic revolt.

He had wiped the spittle from his chin and his shirtfront with Kleenex and was steeling himself for the third try, when the buzzing in his pocket gave him an excuse to call a time-out.

He fumbled the BlackBerry out of his pocket. "Yo," he said, "this is Max."

"Max Christian?" a streety male voice said—Brooklyn, Max guessed.

"That's me. Who's calling?"

"I'm Gus," the voice said. "Your new best friend wants to see you."

"And who would that be?"

"He doesn't like his name said on the phone. He's careful like that. He says if you can't figure out who your new best friend is, you ain't half as smart as he heard you was."

Tina's guy, Max thought suddenly. *Nick. Nick what? Nick Testa.* "Gotcha," he said. "My new best friend want to come by my office?"

"You're kidding, right?" Gus said. "No fuckin' way. You know where the Mariners Inn is at?"

"Yeah, it's four or five blocks from me. I walk by it all the time."

"'Kay, so come by and ask for me. Gus, right? I'm the assistant manager. I'll get you and he together."

"When?"

"How's now? Your friend is not a patient man."

"I'll be there in ten minutes."

"Make it five. He says you don't have to take the long way around no more. Won't be nobody on your ass."

"Huh?"

"He'll tell you about it when you get here. Copy?"

"Copy," Max said. "Be there in five."

Max fast-walked the five blocks to the Mariners, past the polished granite facing, and into a spare but well-lit lobby. At one end, two old-timers in pea jackets were in animated conversation on a settee, and an out-of-town-looking woman sat in a chair, staring at her smartphone. If Testa was indeed in the building, he was somewhere else.

"Gus here?" he asked a black guy at the front desk.

The black guy head-gestured toward a smallish office just behind him. "Gus, you in there?" he asked. "Somebody asking for you."

A thick-set, balding man in shirtsleeves emerged from the office. Max made him to be about fifty. He was shortish, but iron-pumped muscles bulged under his shirt. His forearms and neck were tattooed. His face was deeply creased. His eyes were caution lights: "Don't get too close."

"I'm Gus," he said.

"I'm Max."

"Your friend is up on the mezzanine level. Take those stairs over there."

"You're not gonna put us together?" Max asked. "I don't know the guy."

"He knows you," Gus said. "He preps for meetings. Just head on up."

Max trudged up the stairs to the mezzanine, an L-shaped space fenced in by brass rails and panels of glass. A youngish man with a nose ring was sitting at a public computer, checking his email. A middle-aged woman and her teenage daughter occupied a couch, each of them furiously thumbing out text messages. Max wondered if they were texting one another, saving themselves the discomfort of direct human contact.

His eyes roamed the space and lit finally on a tall, lean

figure sitting alone in a far corner of the L. He looked to be six foot two or three, almost Max's height, and a sinewy 180 pounds. His hair was chestnut brown, threaded with gray. His suit was dark and conservatively cut. His boots were spit-polished to a high gloss. His age was at some unknowable point between forty and sixty. His face was an unlined mask. If eyes were in fact windows to the soul, his were shuttered to the world.

He nodded once, and Max joined him. "Nick?" he said. "Max."

"Have a seat," Nick said, gesturing toward a chair close by his own. "My niece tells me you have a problem might need a closer. That's what I do."

"Yeah, I have a problem. Carlo Paolucci kidnapped my son, Jay, and I've got a little under four days left to get him back alive."

"Don Carlo, yeah. Charlie Beak. Real bad actor, from all I've heard. Tina tell you I have some relatives used to be in that line of work?"

"She mentioned, yeah."

"Right. So an uncle of mine told me some stories about Carlo when he was a young guy coming up that, let's say, made me not care for him. In fact, made me not want any part of that life."

"Like what?"

"Like how he made his bones. He was the boss's son, but to get straightened out—you know, become a made man—he had to prove himself like everyone else by clipping somebody his pop had it in for. Usually, that meant putting two in the back of the head, losing the weapon, and walking away, right?"

"Right," Max said. "I worked two or three of those hits with Tina."

"Yeah, well, that wasn't enough for young Carlo even then. Apparently, he and a couple of his boys took this guy to a steel-pickling plant in Pennsylvania, stripped him bare-ass naked, hung him from a hook, and dipped him slowly into a vat of hydrochloric acid, toes first. My uncle said people could hear the screams across four or five counties."

"And no body to get rid of. Sounds like the Beak—he's told me himself the fun is in the pain."

"As long as it's not his pain, yeah," Nick said.

"As long as it's not his. Right," Max said. "I just spent half the morning watching a video of him torturing my son with a mittful of bullet ants."

"Poor kid—that's some pretty serious hurting. I got bit by one of those suckers on an op once. Took a week for the pain to quit."

"On an op? Where?"

"Government gig," Nick said. "Protecting your freedoms—doesn't matter where. Tell me, though—was this video of your kid date- and time-stamped?"

"Yeah," Max said. "Eight-something last night."

"So at least we know he was alive then. I know you're his dad, but I've gotta be blunt with you—most kidnap victims get killed the first day or two."

"I know that," Max said. "But the Beak has three new toys to play with—my son, my wife, and me. He'll play with us as long as our pain keeps amusing him. When it stops being fun and he's banked our last check, he'll kill us all. But not before then. Be bad for business."

Nick nodded. "So we need a plan to keep that from happening, which is why I'm here. Why don't we start with you telling me the whole story from scratch?"

"Tina filled you in on the basics?"

"Yeah, in outline, but if I'm going to work with you, I need to know everything you remember. I'm pretty sure you know how that goes."

Max smiled a smile of recognition; he was usually guarded with strangers on the farther edges of the law, but he was already beginning to like this Nick from nowhere. "I must have said that same exact thing a thousand times," he said. "Get 'em talking. You listen; you learn."

"I figured," Nick said. "Everything matters. Talk to me."

Over the next three-quarters of an hour, Max recounted all of it in detail: the call in which the Beak said, "I have your son"; the meeting at Caffè Reggio to talk terms; the ransom demands and the daily payments; the Skype call and its aftermath; Jay crunched up in the little-ease for the amusement of his captor; the long, rambling daddy summit over lunch with the Beak, probably in Harlem; the Beak laying out his plans for his son; and the Beak's son's vision for the future of the family and the mob.

"I heard about the kid," Nick said. "Luca, right? What all do we know about him?"

"Not a lot—just the scraps I picked up over that lunch with his dad. He got an MBA from Stanford, and as a graduation present, the Beak set him up with a hedge fund. Which, by the way, it turns out he's really good at—his daddy says the kid is halfway to his first billion."

"Nice money laundry," Nick said. "Keep it in the family."

"That was my take," Max said, "but the Beak swears it's all kosher—says even he's just another investor. Apparently, the plan at first was to keep Luca legit, away from the family business. Didn't quite work out that way—the kid is now neck deep in it, and the Beak's grooming him for boss. To the extent the Paolucci borgata has a business plan, it's Luca's. He wants to take the family corporate. Strip it down to its core competency, in his lingo."

"Which would be drugs?"

"That'd be my guess. But beyond that, I don't know a lot about young Luca."

"I've picked up some," Nick said. "He's got a supersized town house at 221 Beaver Street. I was by there this morning."

"That's down in the financial district. He can walk to work."

"Yeah, down a couple flights of stairs, and he's at his desk, ready to deal. He calls his shop AWE Investments."

"AWE for Agnese Worldwide Enterprises. If you use the acronym, the subliminal message is that this dude is awesome."

"Whatever," Nick said. "Our boy's offices are on the first two floors—ground floor for his receptionist and a couple of security guys and second floor for him, his secretary, and seven or eight traders. Luca and his family bunk upstairs."

"So he lives over the store," Max said. "Just like me."

"Except his store is a lot bigger than yours," Nick said. "Used to be a boutique investment bank. Five stories—set him back ninety million, plus at least that much more to convert it. Fair guess Daddy chipped in."

"A couple of security guys sounds pretty light given who Luca is. The don's son and heir?"

"Appearances," Nick said. "Luca's running a hedge fund, not a numbers bank. He doesn't even use his family name—in his day job, he's Luke Carleton."

"I guess he figured Paolucci wouldn't exactly be a good brand name for a hedge fund," Max said. "When you're running a long con, you don't want a name that raises questions on day one."

"Exactly. Which is also why you go light on security. If you put a guy like Il Lupo out front with that body fat and that pinkie ring he likes, you scare off your investors. Luca's boys are carrying, but they're dressed in slim-line Paul Stuart suits."

Max's eyes widened. "You've been in town two days, and you know all this stuff? I'm impressed."

"Finding a guy who's got a Stanford MBA and runs a hedge fund isn't exactly solving a Rubik's Cube. Not for me anyway—I've got friends in the intel community, guys I did jobs of work for. With the security arrangements, I had a little civilian help. New Yorkers are pretty friendly if you ask them in the right tone of voice and maybe squeeze their balls for emphasis."

"So you asked a New Yorker where Luca's at?"

"Yeah, and it's all good to know," Nick said. "But my guess is, talking to you and Tina, you're thinking extraction, right?"

"Right. Extraction plus execution—I want that motherfucker dead."

"You have a plan?"

"A plan? Fuck, we don't even know where he's holding Jay. We've got a city address for him—he and his security crew have got a duplex in one of those new glass towers poking up all over town. But what we hear, he just overnights there if he's got business in the city. We're pretty sure his real home is somewhere in Westchester County. We just don't know where."

"Guys in his line of work don't leave forwarding addresses," Nick said, "and they don't even buy Snickers bars in their own name, let alone houses. What *do* we know?"

"I had a guy up there, a retired cop, who must've been getting close," Max said. "The Beak's boys caught him working the county clerk's files."

"And?"

Max felt his eyes misting. "They killed him. Blew him wide open with a shotty. Made it look like a home invasion, and Tina's playing it that way for now, for my sake. But it had all the markers of a hit by the Beak's chief enforcer."

"Il Lupo?"

"Yeah. How'd you know?"

"Recon," Nick said. "So we don't know what your guy found, if anything?"

"No. The fuckers took his notepad and his computer, along with everything else that mattered to him."

"So we're thinking extraction, but we don't know where your boy is at. Westchester's a big county. How much time we got?"

"Four days after today is when we're supposed to make the last payment to his account in Vanuatu," Max said. "Soon as it clears is when he's supposed to hand Jay over to me. My guess is he'll arrange a meet somewhere on neutral ground. Only he won't show up—his boys will, and they'll kill Jay and me both. My wife too. We'll all be keeping Jimmy Hoffa company, wherever they buried him."

Nick's eyes roamed the mezzanine, checking, Max guessed, for new faces. The guy at the computer had left. A dad with two kids was channel-surfing on a flat-screen TV in one corner, surrendering finally to the Cartoon Channel. The cast otherwise was unchanged and unthreatening, but Nick lowered his voice when responding to Max.

"I don't know," he said. "You're an ex-cop, right? A decorated ex-cop? I grew up with guys on the Beak's side of the road, and they all said you'd have to be nuts to kill a cop—not 'cause it's wrong; it's just bad for business. We know Don Carlo's not crazy, right?"

"Sick," Max said, "but not crazy. Right. Problem is, he's motivated to take me out—or thinks he is."

"Motivated? By what?"

"Revenge. The Beak's got a serious hard-on for me. He told me at the Reggio meet that I owe him the twenty-five mil for fucking with his drug operations and maybe even bringing that RICO case down on his head. Which, incidentally, I didn't." He paused. "Not directly anyway."

"Is he pissed enough to whack you, though? Get the whole NYPD and the other four New York families mad at him?"

"He must be, 'cause two of his hitters have already tried. One of 'em did this"—Max touched his maimed right ear—"and another carved up my right thigh with a gravity knife. I'd show you that scar, but I'd have to drop my pants to do it, and this doesn't look like that kind of place."

"Okay, so there's that," Nick said. "What we need now is a strategy."

"And time," Max said.

"Four days is plenty—the question is how. Next couple days, keep trying to nail that Westchester location, but I'm thinking we probably need an alternative to extraction. We've gotta assume the don has a lot of security up there, making sure nothing disturbs his sleep, right?"

"I could put together a combat team, if that's what you're thinking. I know guys in Harlem who've been through the wars up there. They wouldn't exactly be Navy SEALs, and they wouldn't have choppers, but they'd be as good as the Beak's hoods in a street fight. Probably better."

"It wouldn't hurt to put that in the works just in case," Nick said. His face was clearly practiced at masking feelings, but Max could read the skepticism in his eyes.

"In case what?" Max asked.

"In case we want to do a feint," Nick said. "A diversion. Move in sometime between two and five in the morning, when even the security guys are kind of dozy. Fire a few shots, get the Beak's soldiers firing back, and get the hell out of Dodge."

"But why a feint? What's that get us?"

"Makes the Beak think he's invulnerable. Guys like him feel like that anyway, and we want him thinking he's just proved it. Like he's taken your best shot and come away unscathed. If we decide on a real extraction, no amateurs, okay? It'd be doable with five combat-trained professionals, and I could put that together with five phone calls. There's guys around here I've worked with in the past."

"I'd cover the costs, however much it takes. But I think you're saying that's not plan A."

"What I'm saying is I'm playing with an idea for plan B. Less direct but equally effective. Maybe more. Give me a day or two to think on it."

"A day or two? Isn't that pushing our luck a little?"

"We've got four. The beauty of plan B is it's simple. Question is whether it's doable. I never go into an operation cold if I can help it—I don't like surprises. Like that hood who's been tailing you. What'd you think—he just all of a sudden lost interest?"

"I was gonna ask you about that," Max said. "Your pal Gus told me I could just walk straight here and not worry about a tail. How'd that happen?"

"Habit you pick up early in Special Forces—you do your recon before you do anything else. I got to town a couple of days before I had Gus call you, so I could check out you and the terrain both. Wasn't hard spotting your shadow hanging out on the corner. When I was a kid, I must've seen a hundred goombahs looked just like him, dressed just like him, and smelled just like him from that cologne they all like."

"And?"

"Well, I admired the rooftop route you took to shake him," Nick said, "but I figured you didn't need the inconvenience with all the bad stuff happening in your life. So I had a little conversation with your tail and his friend Goldilocks up in the apartment across from you—young guy with the ponytail? Funny thing—they both suddenly decided to go away on vacation."

"They went on vacation?" Max said. "Yeah right."

"Right. Didn't say where; didn't even pack. They're just gone."

"Let me guess," Max said. "It was them gave up Luca's whereabouts?"

"Goldilocks, yeah, just before he left. All I had to do was grab him by the hair with one hand and the balls with the other and tell him the only thing behind a ponytail is a horse's ass. Got him singing real quick."

"Soprano?"

"Pretty much."

"And his partner?" Max said.

"A real cement head," Nick said. "All I got from him is 'Nobody tells me nothing.' His parting words, it turned out. Let's say they're both in a better place now."

"But they're replaceable parts. Their listening post is still there."

Nick paused for a moment, looking thoughtful. "Well, no," he said. "A half-gallon screw-top jug of Chianti accidentally got spilled all over that surveillance equipment, so I guess you could say it's on vacation too. Oh, and the Brazilian guy renting them that apartment? We had a little chat on the phone, and he decided he didn't need to rent it to anybody anymore."

This guy, Max thought, gazing silently at Nick and for the first time seeing the danger and the faint pentimento of sadness in his eyes. *This guy—what? This is a guy who's seen a lot—maybe too much. This is a guy not to be fucked with. If I'm right that this is a street beef between me and Charlie Beak, this is a guy I want on my side.*

"So," Max said, breaking the stillness, "if you're aboard, we should probably do up a contract."

"I don't like paper. A handshake's good enough."

"Well, at least give me a number," Max said. "How much you need?"

"Y'know, I'm really doing this for Tina," Nick said. "She thinks very highly of you."

"And I love her, but I pay my people. She tell you my parents were Commies? They never converted me, but there's one Marxist principle I do believe in: the labor theory of value. Give me a number."

"And I believe in honoring fallen warriors. Tell me what you were paying the guy who got blown apart for Beak hunting up in Westchester."

"Five hundred a day, plus expenses. That's my standard for subcontractors, but I'll double it if we get Jay back alive."

"The five's good," Nick said. "We've got a deal."

They shook hands and stood to leave.

"So how do I get in touch with you?" Max asked.

"You don't," Nick said. "I get in touch with you."

"But what if I need to get you fast?"

"Call Gus's cell—he and I are buddies from Fallujah, among other garden spots of the Sandbox. From what Tina tells me, being buddies in a combat zone isn't much different from being partners in a cop car—you're trusting each other with your lives. He fields incoming for me in New York. You got a pad and pen on you?"

Max plucked a Bic and a notebook out of a blazer pocket. Nick dictated Gus's phone number and email address.

"Tina was right. She said you live under the radar," Max said. "I know you're not from here. Where's your home base?"

Nick smiled. "I'll be in touch," he said.

CHAPTER 11

Castello del Becco

"So, love," Meridew said, "how did it go with the mysterious Mr. Testa?"

"I'm not sure," Max said. He'd walked home, shucked his blazer, and draped it over the back of the couch, at the far end from the corner she'd preempted. "Fix you a drink?"

"Sure—a Bristol Cream maybe? Keep you company? You look like you're in the need of solace."

"So do you," Max said. At a glance, she looked relaxed, curled up in jeans and his faded Penn sweatshirt, but he could see the toll of the past couple of weeks in her eyes and her taut attempt at a smile.

He poured the sherry for her and a Mount Gay for himself and slouched onto the couch beside her. "I found myself liking the guy, even though I couldn't really read him. He's a warrior—that much was clear. A real pro. My strong sense is he's seen and done things that aren't necessarily pretty. That's as far as he let me in. Maybe as far as he lets anybody in."

"Does it matter?" Meridew asked. "We're not scripting a bromance here. The only question is, can he help us get Jay back home?"

For a long moment, Max stared into his drink in contemplative silence. He hadn't wanted to frighten Dew with the reality of their situation—with the prohibitive odds against their son's safe return.

"Max? Can he help us?"

"Let's say I think we need him."

"Because?"

"New eyes. Unclouded eyes—ours are clouded by love and dread. I don't think sentiment is part of our boy Nick's makeup." Max sipped his drink. "Like I said, he's a warrior, and we're in a war. Wars are his profession, not mine. I'm just a used-to-be cop."

He felt Meridew's eyes studying him. "But what will he do?" she asked. "Does he have a strategy? A plan?"

Max fell silent again, framing his response. "What I know?" he said finally. "What I know is he doesn't like my plan, which is find the Beak's place and take it by storm."

"Storm it alone?" Meridew said. "That's not a plan; that's a suicide mission, and I wake up the next day a childless widow. No, Max. No."

"I wouldn't be alone. I could raise a combat team."

"How? Where?"

"Harlem," Max said. "I've got friends from the old days. Some of them owe me for knocking down nickel-bag drug collars to misdemeanor possession for use and sparing them time in the joint. A couple of them were muscle for my friend Satin back when he was dealing—guys who know how to fight."

"Did you talk to this Nick about that?"

"Yeah."

"And he said what?"

"He said go ahead—keep looking for Mr. Beak's place and put my Harlem posse together. I've gotta say, though, he seemed mostly amused by the idea. Said he and four special-ops buddies could do an extraction, if that's the direction we go in, but he's cooking up some kind of plan B."

Meridew reached for her drink on the coffee table but left it untouched. "What kind of plan B?" she asked.

"He hasn't told me yet, but my guess? He's thinking of kidnapping the Beak's son and doing a swap."

Once again, Meridew reached for her drink. This time, she took a deep swallow. "Cruelty for cruelty," she said. "Pain for pain. Is that a plan, love, or is it just revenge?"

"It'd be a son for a son, babe," Max said. "If it gets our Jay back, does it matter?"

Meridew sank deeper into the couch cushions and tugged Max's arm around her shoulders. Her eyes were glistening. "No, I suppose it doesn't matter," she said. "Not really. Not if it brings Jay home. But—"

"But what, babe?"

"We're putting our future and Jay's in the hands of a man we don't really know. You remember when we saw *The Threepenny Opera*? How Victoria's messenger comes riding in at the end with a pardon and saves Mack the Knife from the gallows?"

"Sure."

"And do you remember the closing lines? How endings mostly aren't that happy in real life? How Victoria's messenger doesn't come riding often?"

"Yeah, I remember. But Brecht was never exactly what you'd call an optimist." Max smiled. "Last person to quote him to me approvingly was Charlie Beak."

"But are we putting too much trust in this Nick? This stranger from we don't know where? Is he Victoria's messenger riding to the rescue, or are we just hoping he is?"

Max downed the last swallow of Mount Gay from his glass. "You're right, babe," he said. "We don't know him. But the question is, do we trust him? And I guess I do. My instincts tell me he knows what he's doing."

"With four days left?"

"He says that's plenty."

"And we believe him?"

"We have to, babe. He's pretty much the only real hope we've got."

Max reached for his blazer, tugged a fresh Kleenex from an inside pocket, and dabbed away the tears at the corners of Meridew's eyes. He stood. She smiled up at him.

"Gotta go," he said, slipping into the blazer.

"Go where?" she asked.

"Harlem," he said. "See my man Black Satin and get him started raising a war party of middle-aged street bangers."

"So let me get this correct," Satin said on the long drive from Harlem into the exurban reaches of Westchester County. "You axin' me to round up some of my boys for a war that ain't even on the real? They ain't gonna be tryin' to hear that shit from you *or* me."

"I know, I know," Max said, looking for the turnoff for Rye Brook. "But this guy Nick I was telling you about—the special-ops guy? Fought in Iraq and Afghanistan and, I'm pretty sure, some other places he hasn't told me about. He knows war the way you know ball and I know murder policing."

"So he say. Y'all sure you ain't goin' for the okeydoke? Payin' him for what he say he was?"

"Sure as I can be, yeah. What I know is I've got no choice but to trust him. I'm jammed up, I've got less than four days left, and he's the best shot I've got."

Max and Satin had been friends for twenty years, dating to Max's days as a narco undercover in Harlem's Two-Six precinct and Satin's time running a couple of drug corners near St. Nicholas Park. Their common ground had been the park's south basketball court, where Satin was the reigning prince of street ballers and Max was a fresh-out-of-the-academy white boy with black moves. They'd observed a kind of armistice, with Max ignoring some minor infractions and Satin feeding him leads on rival dealers.

Their ways had parted when Max made detective and was reassigned downtown, and Satin was involuntarily relocated upstate to the Clinton Correctional Facility, the Siberia of the state's penal system. But Satin had been determinedly on the straight since his return, and with Max's vision and Edith Clift's philanthropic millions, the Satin Academy for Boys had been created around him. His mission, and the school's, was to give at-risk Harlem kids with little more than empty hoop dreams better grounding for a future beyond the nearest asphalt court and the closest drug corner. Satin's first rule of pedagogy was simple: if you don't do your academics, you don't play.

Max had known he was chasing a fantasy when he'd walked into the office of the Dean of Men that early afternoon and found Satin lounging behind his desk in his old Darktown Strutter warmups and his new LeBron XIII kicks. He'd laid out everything, from the day of the kidnapping to his hookup with the shadowy Nick and their plan for a diversionary raid on the Beak's home base. "Wherever the fuck that is," he'd said. "We're still looking."

"Oh, that ain't y'all problem," Satin had said. "I know where that shit is at."

"You fucking know?" Max had said. "And the FBI and the NYPD don't have a clue? How'd that happen?"

"I been there," Satin had said, smiling at Max's surprise.

"You were there? When? How?"

Satin had flicked an invisible mote from the sleeve of his warmup jacket. "You remember the Strutters?" he'd said. "Clown-show basketball team? I know you do, 'cause you did some games with the white patsy team lettin' us do our tricks and shit."

"Yeah, my job was making you look good. Which, by the way, wasn't easy."

"Seein' as you a fat old man now," Satin said, "I'ma let that pass. You ain't see Satin pickin' on no differently abled individuals."

Max laughed. "I only played that one season like four or five years ago," he said. "Working undercover with my girl Tina, helping you boys figure out who was murdering some of your players. So?"

"So you also recollect how ya boy Massa Beak moved in on that shit and took it over? Turned it into what y'all ofays call a coon show while his boys was peddlin' Oxy an' booger sugar to the rednecks in every runt-ass cracker town we played."

"Yeah, yeah," Max had said, "I recollect. So? Where's this going?"

"Goin' straight up to Mr. Charlie's house, up past Rye Brook, where all them big estates are. We had to go there one day to do a command performance for his son. Boy wadn't yet outa college, but he already had two li'l' kids. Show was for them."

"That's four or five years ago, Satin. You sure you remember where it's at?"

"What I been doin'—stutterin'? Yeah, I remember—you forget where the Empire State Building is at? Satin see a castle, he ain't about to forget it real quick."

"Could you show me on a map?" Max had asked.

"Do better'n that, bruh. I could run you up there right now an' give you a firsthand look, if you got your car. White folks see a nigga drivin' a Benz up in that piece, they gonna call out the National Guard."

"My car's outside."

"Yeah, prolly still there," Satin said. "You parkin' a hoopty like that in the 'hood, the boys gonna think you homeless an' not take nothing past the hubcaps."

It was on the ride up the Hutchinson River Parkway toward Rye Brook that Satin vented his objections to the game plan. "How you think a soldier like U-Haul gonna feel when I tell him we gonna sneak up here middle of the night, set some marshmallows on fire, toss 'em over the fence, an' run away?" he demanded. "Or Death? Or Sweet D? You tell them it's a war, it bed be a war, son. Word."

"They never heard of a feint?" Max asked. "Think rope-a-dope—let a guy think he's winning, and drop him when he lowers his guard. How many fights did Ali win with that? A lot, right?"

"I don't know if I can sell that," Satin said. "I mean, don't think I ain't grateful for all you an' Edith done for me, 'cause it's cookin'. I mean, the academy ain't crankin' out no Einsteins or nothin', but we got one of the lowest dropout rates in the city. Our kids graduate, and the ones goin' to college ain't all goin' on b-ball scholarships."

"Yeah, and Edith and I are both proud of you, Satin. But I didn't come pulling your coat for payback—I came as a friend who needs a favor. Bottom line, the Beak's got my kid, simple as that. I can't go to the cops, I can't go to the feds, and I can't go to the papers. I'm fucking desperate, man."

Satin glanced at him. "Yeah, B," he said. "I see that. I'll think on it."

They drove on in silence for a while, with Satin slumping deeper into the passenger seat as the exurbs got richer and whiter. Max drove. Satin thought.

"Hang a right here," he said suddenly, breaking the stillness. "An' slow down. We almost there."

Max made the turn onto a wooded stretch of blacktop not much wider than a country lane. The streetlights were more numerous and closer together than on the parkway; someone in authority had been persuaded to see to the Beak's sense of security in his own home.

"Slide over to the right," Satin said. "They's a little cutoff up by here where we gonna dump the car an' take a li'l' walk in the woods, you and me. We can hold hands, son, case y'all white ass get scared."

"Fuck you, Satin," Max said. "You bring any bread crumbs to lay a trail case you get us lost? I know I didn't, and we might need some—you know, in case *you* get scared outside your normal urban environment."

"Fuck you back, cuz, and slide off right here."

Max turned off onto a dirt indentation in the woods and parked about ten yards off the road. He got his Leica out of the glovebox, snapped on a telephoto lens, and followed Satin on an easterly course just inside the tree line.

"Walk soft," Satin said. "They used to have them movement things in here."

"Motion sensors?" Max asked.

"Yeah, them," Satin said. "Ol' Massa Beak's boys don't pay close attention to them no more this side of the road. Them motion shits was sendin' up too many false alarms e'ry time a deer came through lookin' to tap some his Bambi-mama booty. Lights start flashin', sirens whoopin', fuckin' Fourth of July poppin', and boss all cranky 'cause he lost some sleep?

Naw, man, them soldiers did what you an' I would do. They unplugged them shits and watched they monitors instead."

"How you know all this? You were only here once."

"I hear shit. You forget I used to work for a dude used to work for Massa Beak? Back in my gangsta days?"

"The dude being the Reverend I. M. Trubble," Max said. "Yeah, I remember. You got caught bringing him a key of yayo and did seven years."

"On a twelve-year bit," Satin said. "And after I came out, I sang at one of his clubs, till he fired my sweet-soundin', old-school-lovin', ghetto-groovin' pipes an' went hip-hop instead. 'For our new white neighbors,' he says. 'They lookin' for authentic negritude.' Fucker gentrified my black ass right out my job."

"And you still hear shit?"

"Yo, I'm still Satin, Harlem still Harlem, an' the wire still the wire. I'ma always hear shit."

They'd trekked nearly a mile, when Satin put a finger to his lips and motioned Max to a stop. "Whoomp, there it is," he said in a half whisper.

"Fuck me," Max said. "Castello del Becco."

What he saw was a large faux-Victorian sprawl of a mansion on a rise maybe a half mile back from the road. Out front, he saw a vast, manicured expanse of green descending to the road, bordered on either side by gated curvilinear driveways and, at the foot of the slope, a high hedgerow. He raised his Leica to eye level and started snapping.

"They's surveillance cameras all up in them bushes, yo," Satin said. "And behind the bushes, they's bob wire you don't want to be touchin', 'less you want y'all ribs barbecued."

"You're saying the wire's electrified?" Max asked.

"You be electi*fried* for real if you touch that shit," Satin said. "Turn them pretty curls into a 'fro jus' like mine. Prolly toast you my color too. But stay cool—I know a funeral director in the 'hood case them downtown undertakers don't want your formerly white ass."

"Yeah, yeah, yeah, I'm fair warned. Thank you very

much. But what do you know about those guesthouses by the driveway gates?"

"They ain't guesthouses, B, they guardhouses. Boss got soldiers stay there six to a house round the clock, twenty-four-seven, seeing whatever them cameras see. Got more muscle an' more iron up in the big house if anybody get past the front line."

Max lowered his camera and blinked at Satin. "Sounds kinda paranoid," he said. "I mean, nobody comes at a don where he lives. If he gets got, it's at some public place where he and his boys loosen their belts and let their guard down. Like Castellano at Spark's Steakhouse or Joey Gallo at Umberto's or—"

"Or Anastasia at a barbershop, yo," Satin said. "You know what the different is? Different is, they all dead, an' Ol' Massa Beak still alive. You know why he still alive? 'Cause he careful e'rywhere he at. Don't make no nevermind, home or away."

"I don't know—I got with him for coffee at Caffè Reggio, and all he brought was Il Lupo."

"And didn't even need that fat-ass fool if you think about it. Didn't take Ol' Massa a whole lot of figurin' to figure you ain't no threat to him—not while he got your boy. But you feel like stayin' safe, we best bounce on out this piece 'fore we get bounced."

"I need to make a couple of calls first," Max said.

"No," Satin said, "you need to get y'all ass back to the car first. Then is phone time, not now."

They tramped back to the car. With some reluctance, Satin slid behind the wheel this time, while Max punched up Ahab on his BlackBerry.

"Hey, boss," Ahab said. "What up?"

"Our mutual friend not only knew where the Holy Grail is; he took me to see it," Max said.

"Yes!"

"I need you to take down the coordinates"—Max dictated them from his GPS app—"and make me the biggest printout you can of the Google satellite photo. I'm also Instagramming you some pictures of the place. I need prints of those too. Copy?"

"Copy. Tell our friend I said hey."

"Will do," Max said. "Anything else stirring?"

"Matter of fact, yeah—I got the Porterfield diamonds. The lady who boosted them is at central booking right now, courtesy of Christian Enquiries."

"Nice work, Sherlock. I'm proud of you. Just make sure you return those diamonds when our brothers in blue get done with them."

"Or before one of our brothers in blue skates with 'em."

"Now, now," Max said. "We used to be police our own selves."

"I get a bonus?" Ahab asked.

"Mm," Max said. "I'll see if we've got a budget line for that."

They both laughed at the notion that such a thing as a budget line or even a budget existed at Christian Enquiries.

Max rang off and dialed Nick's gatekeeper pal Gus.

"I need to get with our friend," he said. "Late afternoon today, like five or six o'clock?"

"Our friend is out of pocket right now."

"See if you can find him," Max said. "Tell him the clock's ticking. Tell him I said, 'At my back, I always hear time's winged chariot hurrying near.'"

"Say what?"

"Never mind—that's just something I heard from a guy I knew in college, Andy Marvell. Just tell our boy it's urgent."

"Like I said, he's out of pocket."

"Try," Max said. He hung up and rang Meridew.

"Hey, babe," he said.

"Max, love. Where are you?"

"Headed home from deep Westchester, where I've seen the McMansion our son is penned up in. Almost made me cry just thinking about it—our Jaybird in a gilded cage. My man Satin guided me there. He knew where it was."

"Please tell me you're not driving while we're talking. I'm scared enough already without having to worry about whether you'll make it home in one piece."

"It's okay, babe. Satin's got the wheel, and he's driving slow as an old white man in Miami Beach who's scared his kids are gonna come down from the city and take his keys away."

"Black man can't be too careful these days," Satin said. "Or any days. Popos out here shootin' niggas for target practice, case you ain't been readin' the papers past the comics."

"You hear that, babe?" Max asked.

Meridew laughed. "I heard it," she said, "and the sad thing is, he's almost right."

"Question now," Max said, "is whether he's gonna round up a team for phase one of our friend's plan." He glanced at Satin. "You should see him, babe," he said. "Pretending he's not hearing me."

Satin held his gaze on the road, his eyes ablaze and his face a taut mahogany mask. "Sometime or another, e'ry black man feel like them Muslim brothas was right when they say y'all white folks ain't but a race of devils," he said. "This one of them times for ol' Satin. Diss me, honky, an' I'ma go all *'Allahu akbar'* on your ass."

"Call you right back, Dew," Max said. He pocketed his phone and reached across to touch Satin's arm. "Satin, man," he said, "I didn't mean—"

Satin pulled off onto the road shoulder and slowed to a stop. "Get out the car," he said.

"Get out of the car?" Max echoed. "It's my fucking car."

"And I'm sayin' get out the car," Satin said, his eyes ablaze. "We gonna settle this right here, right now."

Max stepped out onto the shoulder.

Satin, close behind, advanced toward him with fists cocked for a fight.

Max crouched with his hands up to counter whatever came at him.

They were a left jab's length apart, when Satin started to laugh, a great Niagara of sound exploding from somewhere deep in his belly. He folded Max in a smothering bro hug.

"Jus' fuckin' wid you, Maxi-Pad," he said. "Had ya goin', though, didn't I? All crouched up like you think you Mike

Tyson or somebody. Like you ready to step to ol' Satin an' think you got a chance."

"You saying we're good?" Max asked.

"Yeah, we good, and yeah, I'ma round up a spook army for you if you think it'll help get y'all boy back. I'm a daddy too, yo, an' I know what it's like—a son go missin'."

"Wait—you had a kid kidnapped?"

"In a kind of a way, yeah, you could say that. My baby mama took him down to her mama house in North Carolina when I was doin' my years in the bing, so I ain't see him since he was a shorty. He seventeen now, if he still alive. So yeah, I got an idea how you feelin', and I'ma help any way I can. When you need ya crew?"

"That's the tricky part—the clock's running, so we're gonna have to do this overnight tonight. Can you get ten or a dozen guys together somewhere like around eleven o'clock? Give me a little time to talk about what we're doing and not doing before we roll out?"

Satin smiled. "Eleven at night? That ain't no thang, son— some of my boys just finishin' breakfast round about then. I'll get 'em together in the gym at my school an' let 'em do some hoopin' to warm up."

"Tell 'em to come heavy," Max said. "For the phony war."

"For the phony war. We best get back on the road 'fore I get popped for stealin' a white man's car with the white man still in it. Like I told you a hunnit times, I can't carry no more years."

Max was wiping the dinner dishes dry, when his BlackBerry did an exigent dance in his hip pocket. He fished it up and glanced at the screen. The incoming number was new to him.

"Christian Enquiries," he said. "This is Max."

"It's your friend," Nick's voice said.

"Sorry," Max said. "I didn't recognize your number."

"You're not supposed to. I've got a Burner app on my phone."

"Which does?"

"Which doesn't use the same number twice. Makes it tough on anyone trying to track my calls. So what's on your mind? Gus says you wanted to talk."

"Yeah," Max said. "I got a friend uptown knows our man's home address, and we drove up there for a look today. Same guy's putting together a crew so we can run that operation we talked about. I'm thinking tonight."

"Has to be tonight," Nick said. "Time's marching on, and plan B's almost set to go operational."

"And plan B is?"

"We'll talk about that tomorrow. Tell me what you saw on your trip today."

Max ticked off the points of interest—the mansion on the hill, the treeless sweep of lawn below it, the guardhouses and barbed wire protecting the twin gates, and the wired-up woods out back of the house and across the road out front.

"What have you got for cover?" Nick asked. "My guess is there are motion sensors in those woods across the road."

"There are, but the security guys mostly keep them unplugged. Too many false alarms from the wildlife wandering through."

"Good," Nick said. "So bear in mind, our sole objective here is to make a lot of noise like World War III just broke out and get the hell out with zero casualties. Let the man think the war's over, and he won. You with me?"

"I'm with you."

"Keep your men behind the tree line—they take a step or two out in that roadway, they're dead. You got cover? Use it. Just keep laying down fire till the bad guys start firing back; then get your butts back to your Suburbans and haul ass out of there."

"Suburbans?" Max asked. "Where're we gonna get Suburbans in the middle of the night?"

"Borrow 'em," Nick said. "Return 'em where you found 'em when you get back to town. With the kind of crew you're talking about, grand theft auto's gotta be somebody's MOS."

"Somebody's what?"

"Military occupational specialty. Sorry. I forgot you're a civilian."

Max went silent for a long moment, weighing the proposition.

"What's the matter, man?" Nick said. "You having flashbacks to when you were a cop and jacking a car was bad? With your son's life at stake? You should see what a real war looks like and what you'll do just to survive, let alone win. I gotta ask you—you up for this or not?"

"Yeah, I'm up for it," Max said. "Whatever it takes."

"Good, and come by the Mariners when you get back. We need a sit-down so you can give me an after-action report, and I can brief you on plan B. The balloon is about ready to go up."

CHAPTER 12

Night Moves

"So how'd it go with your midnight riders?" Nick asked.

It was just past four in the morning when Max found him staked out in his favored corner of the mezzanine at the Mariners Inn; the roost gave him sight lines to both wings of the L and the lobby below. Nick looked fresh and clean-shaven. Max was heavy-lidded and stubbly, running on the last of the long night's adrenaline.

"'How'd it go?'" Max echoed. "I know you were skeptical, but my ground-level assessment? It worked. Question is whether it had the impact we were going for."

"It did," Nick said. "Better than we hoped."

"Excuse the language, but how the fuck do you know that?"

"We'll get to that. Tell me what went down."

"Well, let's see." Max paused for the moment it took even a seasoned detective to reduce chaos to some semblance of coherent order. "We borrowed the cars, like you suggested—a couple of Suburbans and an Expedition."

"Tinted windows?" Nick asked.

"Tinted dark. You'd have needed x-ray vision to see in."

"Good. And your troop strength was?"

"Fourteen men, including me and Ahab—he's my partner."

"I know," Nick said.

"I should've figured you would. Anyway, it was mostly guys I knew either from playing ball with 'em or busting 'em on small-time drug charges. Some of 'em both. My man Black Satin vouched for the ones I didn't know."

"These are street bloods, right?" Nick asked. "You sure you can trust 'em? What we don't need is a bunch of corner boys telling the world their war stories."

"These guys?" Max said. "These guys are men in their thirties and forties, which qualifies them as survivors in the world they come out of. They're alive today partly because they know not to tell their war stories."

"You're saying we have to trust 'em, so we trust them. Okay—too late to change up now anyway. So tell me your war story."

"Right. So we do a shape-up in the gym at Satin's school and divide up into three teams—I got one, Satin's got one, and Ahab's got one. We inventory the weapons—mostly handguns, one Bushmaster, one shotty. Oh, and this one guy, Li'l' Moses, shows up with a couple of stun grenades and a paper bag full of earplugs—you believe that?"

"M84s," Nick said. "Flashbangs. What'd Moses do—sneak 'em home from Iraq? Boost 'em from an armory?"

"Says he bought 'em online a couple months ago and was just waiting for the right time to try 'em out," Max said. "And you know what? I did some Googling when I got home, and it turns out you *can* get those babies online. Not even on the dark web—right out in the open, like you were buying 'em on Amazon or eBay."

"Okay. And?"

"We get in the trucks and head up into Beak country a little past oh-two-hundred hours. Minimal traffic—takes us just under an hour. We get there; the only lights on are in the two guardhouses and the two wings running off the big house. We figure that hour, Charlie and Mizzus Beak are either asleep or intertwined—more likely asleep at their age. We park the cars and deploy behind them for cover. Li'l' Moses low-walks across the road, right up to the hedgerow, with the grenades. We good so far?"

"Good enough. And?"

"We do what we came to do: we start shooting. We take out the streetlights first and then just fire blind into the hedges, aiming high 'cause the plan was just make noise, right? So we make a lot of noise for maybe a minute or a minute and a half, and we're hearing the Beak's boys pouring out of the guardhouses, yelling and milling around and shooting back our way as blindly as we're shooting theirs. Sirens are whooping, and the whole scene is floodlit. Which is when Li'l' Moses tosses the grenades into the compound, one by each guardhouse, and *kaboom!* They go off with a huge bang and a flash of light."

"That's what those babies do," Nick said. "A hostile's anywhere near one of 'em, it's like he's standing next to a jet engine and staring straight into the sun at the same time— he's a temporarily deaf, blind stumblebum. He'll get over the worst of it pretty quick, but it'll take him out of the game long enough for you to make your move."

"And our move was hauling ass out of there, like we discussed. We hear the Beak's boys stumbling around, cussing, bumping into each other—they're out of the game, like you said, but reinforcements start coming down the hill from the big house with AKs and M-16s, which is when we climb in our cars and head the fuck out, pedal to the metal. You know, discretion being the better part of valor and all."

"Well played," Nick said. "You take any casualties?"

"One sprained ankle during the getaway was all. I mean, other than a few bug bites and some hurt feelings that we weren't in it to win it. They got over that when they got their pay envelopes. Old Dr. Benjamin is still the great healer of bruised egos."

"You did good, Max," Nick said, "and I brought the proof." He dipped into his breast pocket for a digital voice recorder and a pair of earbuds and passed them to Max. "Check this out," he said, "but use the buds."

"Why? There's no one else here this hour."

124

"Correction: you don't see anyone else here. Use the buds. They're cherry, if that's what you're worried about. Never been used. You won't catch anything."

Max planted the buds in his ears, clicked the Play button, and found himself listening to the unmistakable voice of Charlie Beak.

"Sorry to wake you at this ungodly hour, Luca, but never forget: you're my consigliere as well as my son. We've had a bit of an issue up here that I thought we should discuss."

"What is it, Pop? What kind of issue that we need to talk about it at—what is it?—four in the morning?"

"*Issue* is perhaps too strong a word—*opera buffa* would be more appropriate. I was downstairs in the kitchen for my usual midnight snack—"

"Bad habit, Pop. You really should try to break it."

"I know, I know. But as I started to say, I was in the kitchen, when I heard gunfire and a couple of loud explosions on our grounds. I immediately called Lupo, but he and my home guards were already headed down to the gates. There had been an attack, Luca. On my home. On our home, which will one day be yours."

"And you call that a comic opera? What's funny about that?"

"What's funny is that it was our friend Detective Christian's feeble attempt to storm the gates and free his son. What's truly funny is that he tried to do it with a dozen street hoodlums. Less than hoodlums, actually—*melanzane*. Dark people. Apes."

"And what happened, Pop? What did they do?"

"They came, they fired a few blind shots into the foliage, and they lobbed a couple of cannon crackers over the hedges. But as soon as we began shooting back, they ran as the *mulignane* always run—cowardice is in their blood. I laughed myself silly watching the surveillance tapes. I could see our legendary hero detective fleeing into the night even faster than his moolie brigade."

"Any of our people get hurt?"

"One *cugine* managed to shoot himself in the hip in the confusion. That was it."

"But what are you going to do to punish this *fanook* detective for his gall? You said you called me as your consigliere. My advice to my don is you can't let it pass—you've got to do something."

"Do what? If we terminate him now, we lose the seven and a half million he still owes us. If you have a cash cow, milk it dry—wasn't that one of the axioms you brought home from Stanford?"

"You're right, Pop, but would you just consider giving your bullet ants another go at the kid? Maybe on Skype this time, so his daddy sees it live."

"I thought of that, but experimenting on the boy no longer amuses me. It's too easy. He has a little girl's threshold of pain. Where's the pleasure for me?"

"So you intend to do nothing at all?"

"No, Son, I intend to do something. I intend to pour myself a grappa, finish my snack, and celebrate."

"I'm still not seeing anything to celebrate, Pop."

"You should. Our enemy has played his last card, and it turned out to be a joker. The joke is on him. He has no recourse except to meet his last payday this Friday, after which he and his crybaby son will simply disappear."

"Okay, but—"

"And there's another reason to rejoice in the news of the day, consigliere mio. Our treasonous friend Reverend Trubble? It seems his G-man protectors allowed him a carry-out dinner from Molto Mangiare in Carroll Gardens, an establishment favored by many of our associates. I'm told it had always pleased him, as a non-Sicilian, to feel accepted there."

"And?"

"Sadly, the reverend had a violent allergic reaction to his feast after only a few bites and passed away before his federal guardians could revive him. *Che tragedia*, no? I must send flowers to his widow."

"And send some to the federales too, Pop. I think their RICO case just died."

126

Father and son were still laughing when Max clicked the Off button.

"What the fuck?" he said.

Nick said nothing.

"Confirms what I thought all along," Max said. "Jay and I get disappeared the day Charlie B. banks the last payment."

"Looks like that's the plan," Nick said.

"And probably Meridew, Ahab, and anybody else the Beak even thinks might know the backstory."

"That's what I would do if I was him."

"How'd you get this?"

"While you were busy playing cowboys and Indians up in Westchester, I was getting to know the ways of the Paolucci family."

"Doing a little cultural anthropology?"

"In my world," Nick said, "we call it infiltration."

"As in?"

"As in letting myself into Luca's place awhile after the last lights went out, around one in the morning. Had a look around and learned all kinds of interesting stuff."

"For example?"

"He likes Armani suits and Testoni shoes—high-end goods. He favors 2000 Bordeaux for himself and his clients, but he stocks some Sicilian reds, presumably for when Pop drops by. His wife, Elena, has a whole walk-in closet just for shoes. Luca does blow in his office—his stash and his spoon stay in his top right desk drawer. Let's see—what else?" He paused. "Oh yeah, Elena's cell has a bunch of horny texts from somebody just signs himself G. She's also got every Monday, Wednesday, and Friday booked for shopping from two to four in the afternoon. My guess is this G's shopping with her, only *shopping* isn't what they called it in our day."

"Luca's got competition?" Max asked.

"Looks like it. He and Elena sleep in separate bedrooms, so they're not what you'd call a cuddly couple."

"And you found all this out without waking anybody up?"

Nick smiled. "That's why they call it special ops. I put taps on their landlines, got their iPhone numbers, and planted

AV devices upstairs and downstairs so we can keep track of where they are and when. Neither of them stirred. And when I was done there, I did the Beak's apartment uptown."

"How the fuck did you get past their security guys?"

"When you do government work, you learn stuff," Nick said. "Uncle Sam's a pretty good teacher, and I was a dedicated student."

"And nobody tried to stop you?"

"One guy at the Beak's place."

"And?" Max asked.

"Him?" Nick said. "Oh, he's on vacation. Didn't say where."

Max handed the recorder and the earbuds back to Nick. "But this was a phone call I was listening to, right?" he asked. "You're not saying this little father-son chat happened on landlines, right?"

"No, they're smarter than that," Nick said. "Junior needs the landline for the legit side of his hedge fund business, but otherwise, they've switched to smartphones like everybody else. Makes 'em feel bug-proof."

"Evidently, they're not," Max said. "Not from what I just heard anyway. How'd you manage that?"

"You used to be a cop—you never heard of Stingray?"

"Sure. Gizmo that intercepts cell calls, right? But I heard they were fucked when everybody started using 3G and 4G phones."

"That was before the Hailstorm upgrade to Stingray. You get a brand-new, state-of-the-art phone and think you're immune, but you're not. Hailstorm is listening."

"And you've got one of those babies?" Max asked. "I heard they cost over a hundred large."

"Well over—that's if you're paying for it."

"You didn't?"

"Didn't have to. A guy I did a government job for owed me a favor and gave me one a while back. Said it fell off the back of a Humvee."

Max chuckled. Nick kept a poker face.

"Where'd you set up?" Max asked.

"Vacant office building across the street, scheduled for

demolition starting in a couple weeks," Nick said. "Making way for—guess what—another condo tower. I found an empty front office and moved in. Just in time to catch that call, it turned out."

"So where do we stand now?" Max asked. "I mean, we've only got three days left."

"Three days is enough," Nick said. "My guess is you've figured out what our basic play is. Correct?"

"I think so. We snatch the Beak's kid and arrange a one-for-one exchange, Luca for Jay, right?"

"Right. I hoped we could do our thing this morning, but I ran into a complication on my Beaver Street recon run. Seems our boy has a safe room maybe ten or twelve steps from his office, with what looked like a TL-30-rated door—thick steel inside a fireproof ceramic shell. Can't blow it; can't burn through it. He gets in there, we're fucked."

"Which is what he'll do if he catches even a whiff of trouble, right?"

"Right. So we're gonna take an extra day today for me to run a little short con on young Luca. I call him as soon as he hits his desk in the morning. I tell him I represent a Florida businessman with ten million he'd like to invest—'Discreetly, if you get my meaning,' I'll say. If he hesitates, I let slip that my guy is 'a friend of ours in Miami.' That should get me in the door by tomorrow afternoon."

"You really think so?" Max asked. "Wouldn't he check around first? Do his due diligence?"

"Oh yeah, he'll want a name," Nick said. "As it happens, I've got a name I can give him."

"Another friend who owes you a favor?"

"Another friend owes me a big favor, and I called it in. A connected guy. Luca calls him, and he says, 'Yeah, I'm the guy with the ten mil, and yeah, this guy you're talking to? He's my man. He'll make the delivery, and you won't even have to count it.'"

"And Luca will see you on this one guy's word?"

"Oh, he'll see me—bet it. I know where these guys' G-spots are. I know *them*. You mention ten million and maybe let 'em think it's yayo money needs laundering, they'll be panting like a rabbit in heat. They're not calling their daddies or anyone else for permission—they're gonna let me in the door."

"And?"

"I sweet-talk our boy a little—massage his ego, tickle his greed, win his confidence. Soon as I feel a tug on the line, I tell him I need to talk to my principal tonight, but let's get together again first thing tomorrow morning and deal."

"So while you're greasing Luca, I'm doing what?"

"Right now? Get some rack time—you look like shit."

"You don't have to ask twice."

"What about your partner? He got the stones for what's next?"

Max smiled. "I didn't hire Ahab for his looks," he said.

"Good," Nick said, "'cause we'll need you rested and him ready when we go operational."

"Which is when?"

"Tomorrow," Nick said. "Here's the plan."

Max hadn't wanted to waken Meridew when he got home just before sunrise, so he'd stretched out on his office couch, and he was just getting to sleep when he heard a clinking sound across the room. He snapped awake, sat upright with his hand on his holstered SIG, and saw Camus's extraterrestrial shade stirring up a short pastis.

"What're you doing here?" Max demanded. "You fire my ass twice, and you're gonna come back uninvited for free drinks?"

"You best chill, B, an' listen," Camus said, "'cause I got shit to say and no more'n fi' minutes to say it in. I was over in Ghost Town, drinkin' Colt 45s wid my boy Herman."

"Herman who? Herman Melville? Hermann Hesse? Herman Wouk?"

"Wouk? Honky, please. Naw, it was Melville, and I have much love for the man, but he do get a li'l' wordy sometime— thass why don't nobody but grad students read *Moby Dick* twice, and some ain't even got through it the first time. But what I found out? When he get his mouf goin' on a hunnit like he do, you can slide on out an' give y'all ears a little rest. You got at least fi' minutes 'fore he notice you ain't there."

"And we've blown more'n a minute of that already," Max said. "So what's so urgent you came all the way from Ghost Town to tell me?"

Camus sipped his pastis without removing the stub of the Gauloise eternally aglow in the corner of his mouth. "I wasn't likin' what you and ya boy Nick was layin' down," he said. "Get pain, give pain? We got to be past that, son."

"What's your problem, Al? Is it Nick? I like the guy—case closed. Or is it Nick's plan? At least he's trying to help me get my son back, which is more than I can say about some of my so-called friends."

"If you mean me, you trippin', B, 'cause I been tryin' to help. It's just we know they's evil in the world, and you an' ya boy Nick gonna talk 'bout adding to it? Evil for evil? Crime for crime? You kidnap my boy, so I kidnap yours? An' if that ain't bad enough, you know somebody gonna get deaded behind that shit. Could be your son. Could be you."

"Life is risk, Al—you taught me to accept that fact. Taught me to embrace it—embrace the fact that the world is absurd, which means shit happens. And if the risk is kill or be killed, don't I have to embrace that too? I don't see another choice."

"They's always a choice, son. Bad plus bad don't never add up to good."

Max considered pouring himself a drink but decided against it; the only painkiller he really wanted was sleep. "Y'know, Al," he said, "I'm not much of a Jew, but wasn't Moses on to something when he talked about an eye for an eye?"

"And I ain't any kind of religious, but wadn't the boy Jesus on to something, talkin' 'bout doin' unto others? Look to me like you standin' at the door to unhappiness. You ain't got to knock."

"Unhappiness is where I'm at right now," Max said. "I've gotta do what I've gotta do."

"I see I ain't helpin'," Camus said, "so I'ma get on back to Ghost Town 'fore Herman realize I been gone. Got that forty gettin' warm on the bar."

"Later?" Max said.

"Maybe, maybe not," Camus said, dissolving into the spring glow outside on Eighteenth Street. "Like my boy Fats Waller say, 'One never knows, do one?'"

CHAPTER 13

The Package

Max let himself into the back entrance to the abandoned office building, climbed two steep flights of stairs, and found Nick sitting on a packing crate in the office he'd commandeered two nights earlier. He was dressed for business, dark-side Miami style: a beige linen suit, a wide-collared black shirt open to the third button, and a gold chain ornamenting his furry chest. Behind him, a shortish young woman with shoulder-length ash-brown hair stood gazing out a grimy window toward Luca Paolucci's stronghold across Beaver Street.

"Dani," Nick said, "this is Max, the guy I was telling you about. Max, Dani. She's gonna be helping us out today."

Dani turned toward Max and studied him with dark, unsmiling eyes. She was no more than five feet four or five, he guessed, a bit small for a member of his assault team, but under her severe navy pantsuit, her build was wiry, and her grip when they shook hands was surprisingly strong.

"So where's your sidekick?" Nick asked. "We're bumping up against H hour, and we don't have all afternoon for this. My appointment with Luca's at two thirty. Elena's out, probably with this G guy, shopping till they drop. But the kids get home from school a little after three, which gives us a half hour max to work with."

Max pulled another crate next to Nick's and sat down. "Half hour should be enough," he said. "You think?"

"It's plenty if everything goes well—the whole op shouldn't take more'n ten or fifteen minutes. Less if I had my own crew with me. Trouble is, everything doesn't always go well, and showing up late isn't exactly a good start."

"Chill, Nick," Max said. "Ahab'll be here."

"He bringing the Tasers?"

"Yeah, on loan from Tina. She says they fell off the back of an emergency services truck."

Nick smiled. "My girl," he said.

"Although she'll be in a world of hurt if we don't pull this off," Max said.

"We will. No sweat."

Max glanced over at Dani, who was back at her vigil in the window. The grime on the glass turned the sunlight into an aura of gray around her.

"So who's Dani?" Max asked, lowering his voice almost to a whisper.

Nick sat silently for a moment, studying the worn linoleum flooring between his feet. Max expected the usual response, a clipped answer, or maybe no answer at all; he'd become aware that Nick's world was normally a gated compound closed to outsiders. But when Nick looked up, his thousand-mile stare said that Max had touched a raw place, an incompletely healed wound.

"Dani?" Nick said. "I guess you could call her my godchild. My legacy."

"Your legacy?"

"Yeah, from her dad. Guy named Edoardo Longo—went by Eddie. Him and me—we were like brothers, two guys from the island making a buck fighting other people's wars."

"From the island? What, Long Island?"

Nick laughed a one-beat laugh. "No, Sicily. We were both born in the USA, but the island's in our blood. We were bros in the Sandbox and mercs together in a couple of civil wars in Africa, whichever side paid better."

"You're saying after Iraq and Afghanistan, you were a soldier of fortune?"

Nick looked at Max. His eyes were shining. "Soldier of misfortune, more like. Bad life choice, and bad trip for the both of us, except I made it home, and Eddie didn't. Tough guy—former marine, ex–French Foreign Legion—but he caught one in the back of the neck in Congo-Brass and died in my arms."

"Rough," Max said.

"Worse than rough. Eddie'd married a Corsican girl, but she died of breast cancer while we were playing soldier, and their kid was living in whatever passes for foster care in Corsica."

"The kid was Dani?"

"The kid was Dani. I promised Eddie I'd look after her. I don't know if he heard me or not, but that promise mattered to me."

"Looks like you kept it," Max said. "She's here."

"I look out for her," Nick said. "She looks out for my restaurant."

"Wait—you have a restaurant?"

"Yeah, after Eddie, I decided, *Fuck it. I've got PTSD bad enough already, and I don't have room on my skin for any more scars. Nick Testa is hereby done with wars.* I had some mustering-out money put away. I get a PI license and make some more bodyguarding a couple of gazillionaire businessmen. One was probably legit. The other was kind of iffy, but asking questions can be bad for business, so I didn't ask any. What mattered was both these guys were rich and paranoid, which made for some nice paydays. Very nice."

"Nice enough for you to open a restaurant?"

"Nice enough for a down payment on a bankrupt seafood joint in Palm Beach. I redo it myself with a couple buddies and reopen it as Nick & Eddie's. You're ever down that way, dinner and drinks are on the house, whether I'm there or not. Dani's the manager, and my friends are her friends."

"But what we're doing here isn't restaurant management. Can she handle her end? Helping effect the entry and delivering the package?"

Nick smiled. "You don't know Dani," he said. "She's Eddie Longo's daughter, Siciliana to the bone. You're about to be surprised at what she can do."

The two men were sitting on the crates, when they heard Ahab's footsteps on the back stairs.

"So Palm Beach is where you live?" Max asked.

"No," Nick said. The gate to his private world had closed again.

"Sorry I'm late," Ahab said, letting himself into the room. "Traffic's really fucked."

"Okay, forget it," Nick said. "It's five minutes to H hour. Everybody got their assignments straight?"

"We're good, right, guys?" Max said. Dani and Ahab nodded.

"Which means everybody knows no gunplay unless it's absolutely necessary?" Nick said. "Gunfire draws cops, which we don't need."

"Like I said," Max replied, "we're good."

"Okay, I'm out of here. Max, keep your cell on, and be ready to move when you hear from me."

Max joined Dani at the window and watched Nick stride briskly across Beaver Street, up a couple of steps, and through the portals to Agnese Investments. A minute passed and then another and another. Max pressed his BlackBerry closer to his ear. He heard an inaudible exchange at the reception desk, the grinding sound of an old-model elevator starting upstairs, and another half-heard exchange with the secretary posted outside Luca's office. A door opened and closed.

Yet another minute oozed by.

"I'm in," Nick's voice said.

"Copy that," Max said. "We're right behind you."

"Two of the Beak's soldiers have the lobby—one next to

the girl behind the reception desk and the other floating. You know what to do."

"We're on it," Max said. He turned to the others. "We're looking at a floater, a sitter, and the girl. I got the floater. Ahab, you deal with the sitter. Dani, I don't mean to be sexist, but we're looking at girl-on-girl action here. You've got the receptionist."

When they'd crossed the street to the doorway of Luca's redoubt, Max burst in first, his Taser cradled in his two hands.

"Freeze, motherfuckers," he ordered. "Police. Hands where I can see 'em."

For a split second, everybody froze, long enough for Max to zap the floater and drop him to his knees. The sitter was rounding the end of the reception desk and going for his gun, when Ahab tased him. The gun clattered onto the Moorish-tiled floor. The sitter went into a brief electrified dance, pitched forward, and wound up face down on the tiling.

Across the lobby, the young ash-blonde receptionist was reaching into her desk drawer, when she felt Dani's .22 pistol pressed to the back of her head.

"What's your name, girlfriend?" Dani asked.

"Uh, Angie," the girl said.

"And what are you reaching for, Angie? A button? A gun?"

Angie went stock still, her fingers just inside the drawer. Dani slammed it shut with bone-splintering force. Angie's mouth opened wide in a silent scream. Dani stuffed it with a thick wad of Kleenex from a dispenser on the desk, yanked the phone loose from its mooring, and bound Angie's hands behind her with the cord.

"We own downstairs," Max said on his cell.

"Okay," Nick said. "I'm sitting on the package, but I need you and Ahab up here to pacify the area. Dani can handle downstairs."

"Done," Max said. He pocketed his Blackberry, turning to his team. "Ahab, lock these humps in the guardroom, and come with me."

"Angie too?"

"Angie too. Dani, you're the new receptionist. If anyone comes in wanting to see Luca, he left suddenly on a business trip—didn't say where, didn't say when he'd be back."

Dani nodded. Max and Ahab headed for the elevator and punched the button for the second floor.

When they stepped out, the upstairs security man disengaged from his desk and crossed the floor to meet them. To Max, he looked young for a Paolucci soldier—so young he'd still be carded at a bar. But he carried his slate-gray Brooks Brothers suit well, and his manner was smooth; Max guessed he'd been chosen more for his executive-suite bearing than for his combat skills.

"May I help you, gentlemen?" he asked.

"We're here to see Mr. Carleton," Max said. "It's a business matter."

"He's with a client right now. Do you have an appointment?"

"I thought I did," Max said, fishing his BlackBerry out of his breast pocket. "Let me double-check to make sure I've got the right day." He punched up his calendar app. "I left my glasses at home, and I'm blind without them," he said. He thrust the phone toward the boy gatekeeper. "Could you help me out?"

The kid peered at the screen. "All I'm seeing for today is 'op,'" he said, handing the phone back to Max. He was unaware of Ahab's Ruger .380 semiauto till he felt its muzzle in his right ear. "Fuck," he said.

"No, *fucked* would be a more accurate choice of words," Max said, "'cause that's what you are. What's your name, kid?"

"Giacomo," the kid said. "Jackie." He was standing at rigid attention—maybe, Max guessed, so as not to show he was trembling.

"You don't ever go by G, do you, son?"

The kid blushed.

"You're late for shopping, aren't you?"

"Huh?" the kid said, turning a deeper crimson.

"Be a good boy, and we won't rat you out," Max said. "But I'm still gonna have to frisk you."

A brisk pat-down yielded one pistol in a shoulder holster,

a second jammed under the kid's waistband in back, and a straight razor nesting in one calf-high sock. Max emptied the guns and pocketed the razor.

"That's a lot of hardware to be carrying around a respectable Wall Street investment house," he said. "I guess you're just not a people person, G—am I right?"

"Fuck you," the kid said.

"Ahab, cuff this skel, and take him in the back office over there." Max nodded toward the door to the staff work space. "He acts up, put him to sleep, and tell everybody else in there to shut down their computers and sit quietly in their cubicles with their hands folded in front of them."

"Done, boss," Ahab said.

"Oh, and collect their cells, and yank their landlines, just in case anyone decides to get fresh and dial 911."

"What about her?" Ahab asked, gesturing toward Luca's secretary. She was twenty-fiveish and slender, with streaked blonde hair worn straight and long in the favored style of the day. Maybe, Max thought, Luca's wife wasn't the only one in the family who liked shopping. Maybe she had competition too.

Max fixed the secretary with a dark stare. "What's your name, young lady?"

"Lynn," she said. "But what—"

"Lynn," he said, "you look like a smart girl. Are you gonna be a well-behaved girl too and go keep the number crunchers company?"

"Like I have a choice," she replied.

She reached for her bag. Max lifted it gently from her hands, dipped into it, and came up with an iPhone and a .22-caliber pistol. "I'm afraid I'll have to hold on to these for now," he said, "but whatever you're thinking, we're not robbers—we're here on business. Your bag will be on your desk when you come out, whenever that is. Promise."

He watched Ahab force-marching the two POWs across an expanse of spotless white carpeting and into the boiler room, where the nerds were. When the door had closed behind them, he stepped into Luca's office.

Luca was sitting behind a large faux-Renaissance desk,

his mouth plastered shut with duct tape, his hands zip-tied to the arms of his Aeron chair. To Max's eye, he was the Beak minus the beak, with a nose a bit too radically downsized by cosmetic surgery. He was otherwise a younger likeness of his father, with the same fine features, gelid eyes, and sharp chin. His bronze-dyed hair was combed straight back in the Gordon Gekko style; the gel holding it in place glistened in the harsh fluorescent light.

"All quiet out there?" Nick asked. He was standing behind Luca with the hand holding his subcompact Beretta dangling at his side.

"All quiet," Max said. "Young Luca's keepers downstairs are having their afternoon naps."

"Okay, we've got under five minutes to work with. You know computers, right?"

"Well enough, yeah."

"Well enough is good enough—I don't even own one. See what's on his while I check the paper files. Oh, and watch out for puddles—Prince Charming here pissed his pants when I came in here carrying a gun instead of ten mil in a garbage bag."

"Just pissed?" Max asked. "Could have been worse, right?"

"Right. A lot worse."

Nick attacked the filing cabinets, tossing folder after useless folder onto the pricey Mamluk carpet. Max rolled Luca and his chair aside and stood pecking at the keyboard of the desktop PC. A fast search of folders on the hard drive yielded nothing that looked useful. He tried a backup hard drive and came up empty again.

"Fuck me," he said. "You find anything, Nick?"

"Nothing," Nick said. "I don't know dick about hedge funds, but this stuff all looks legit to me. I'm thinking we'd better settle for what we've got, which is Luca, and get our butts outa here."

"Gimme one sec," Max said. He started rummaging through the desk drawers one by one. Mostly, he found the detritus common to executive desks, but in the top drawer, next to an open antique snuff box filled with yayo, he spotted a

128-gig flash drive. He plugged it into Luca's PC and scanned the contents. "Bingo!" he said. "And the crowd goes crazy!"

"C'mon, Max, no fucking around," Nick said. "Soon as I get the package unwrapped, we move. Capisce? The van's already here."

"No, wait. We've got something here," Max said. "There's a bunch of files with names starting AWE."

"Daddy's corporate front? Agnese whatever?"

"Gotta be," Max said. "They're all encrypted, so we'll need a password to open them, but I'm thinking we've got the goods."

"I'm pretty sure Junior here will give us the password, won't you, sonny?" Nick said. He'd untethered Luca's hands from the chair arms and was peeling the tape from his mouth. "After a little attitude adjustment if he doesn't play nice."

"Fucked if I'll tell you anything," Luca said, sounding brave but looking scared. "Do you people know who I am? Who my father is? How he deals with people like you?"

"We know," Max said. "That's why we're here. What's the password?"

"You think I'd give that up? What're you idiots gonna do if I don't—kill me?"

"It's crossed my mind," Max said.

"But you can't do it, can you, Detective?" Luca said. "That's right. I know who you are, and I can guess why you're here. You're hoping to trade me for your son, right? But I'm worth nothing to you dead. My pop wouldn't trade your son live for his own son's corpse. Think about it."

"You've got a point there, kid," Nick said. "But what if we don't kill you? What if we just blow out your kneecaps with a Greener instead?"

"A Greener?" Luca asked.

"A sawed-off pump-action shotgun if you're really asking," Nick said. "I used to carry one in my backpack while defending the American way in the Sandbox. If this baby does your knees, it'll hurt like hell for a hell of a long time and maybe leave you in a wheelchair or a walker the rest of your life.

But you'll still be breathing, which makes you tradable merchandise. Think about that."

"You wouldn't do that," Luca said.

"Try me," Nick said. "I'll be out of jail before you're out of the hospital—that's if I'm dumb enough to get caught."

"My pop's men would hunt you down and kill you," Luca said. "Slowly, the way Pop likes. He's been called a student of pain."

"So have I," Nick said. "They teach it at Special Forces school. Want a taste?"

Panic flared in Luca's dark eyes. "No," he mumbled.

"I didn't think so. Cuff this brat, Max. We're headed out."

"Where am I going?" Luca asked, his voice a whimper.

"A little boating holiday," Nick said. "Probably not the kind you're used to—you won't be doing any island hopping. No tiki bars, umbrella drinks, or hot babes by the pool—none of that. But you'll get to like IV nutrition—I mean, once you realize that's all the nutrition you're gonna get. No first-class cabins and no captain's table on this ship."

He half shoved and half dragged Luca to the elevator. It was only big enough for two, so Max took the stairs and beat them to the lobby.

"You're up," he told Dani at the reception desk. "Nick's on his way down with the package."

She extended her hand for another bone-crunching shake. "Nice meeting you," she said, already in motion toward the door. "See you whenever."

CHAPTER 14

The Deal

Standing on the front steps, Max watched Nick shove Luca roughly across the pavement toward the gray van idling at the curb. The lettering on the side read, "The Bug Brothers—We Remove Pests." A few passersby stopped to stare, and one of them—a fiftyish man in a blue blazer and gray flannel pants—moved toward Luca as if to intervene.

"I know this man," he said, his accent vaguely British. "I have investments with him. I've an appointment with him tomorrow. I demand to know what's going on here."

Nick reached into his breast pocket for a card case, flipped it open, and flashed it at the intruder.

"This is a national security matter," he said. "I need you to back off now, sir—unless, of course, you want to take a trip abroad with your friend here. The trip's called extraordinary rendition. I don't think you'd care for it."

The man backed away, his eyes wide, and the cluster of spectators receded like ebb tide behind him. The driver's-side door of the van popped open. Nick's buddy Gus stepped out, hefted Luca into the back, and climbed in beside him. Dani took the wheel, and the van glided into the stream of westbound traffic.

Max and Nick stood watching till it had disappeared

around a corner three blocks away. "Okay," Nick said, "it's cleanup time. Tell Ahab he can come on out now."

"Leave the POWs locked up?"

"No need. If there's fifteen civilians, they'll tell the cops thirty different stories."

"Yeah," Max said, "trust me. I know how that goes. One guy'll say it was a lone seven-foot Negro with a sawed-off, and another guy'll go, 'No, it was six guys from ISIS with scimitars,' and it'll wind up in the files as 'person or persons unknown.' But what about the Beak's wiseguys?"

"My guess?" Nick said. "They'll disappear. Put yourself in their place—would you want to be the one telling your don his son's been snatched, and you didn't go down fighting to save him? I know I wouldn't. I'd be La Guardia–bound right now, booking the next flight anywhere."

Max laughed. "I guess we're okay," he said. "For now at least."

"You see me running?" Nick said.

"I gotta stay till Ahab's out—he's my ride. But tell me— what's this business about Luca's boat trip?"

"That?" Nick said. "My buddy Gus has an old boat— bought it secondhand when he came home from his second deployment with a discharge, a Heart, and a couple of missing fingers on his left hand, which you no doubt noticed. He used to take it out weekends, but it was getting kind of cranky, and he mostly keeps it berthed up at a marina on City Island. These days, he only uses it for special occasions."

"Like this?"

"Like this," Nick said. "We'll park Luca there for the next thirty-six to forty-eight hours. Gus'll look in on him and see he gets his IV feed and a trip to the head twice a day. Should be enough, although after today, I'm not sure of his toilet training."

"And you'll have Gus email me photos soon as he can? Better yet, a video? The Beak will want proof of life."

"Done, my friend. I've gotta get going, but you'll need this." Nick handed Max an iPhone. "It's Baby Luca's," he said. "It's got his dad on speed dial. Use it when you contact him—he'll see the number and think it's his kid calling."

"You think he'll buy the deal?" Max asked.

"Wouldn't you in his shoes? You've got his son and his trade secrets. He doesn't have a whole lot of choice."

"I'll have his trade secrets if we get that password."

"Gus'll get it," Nick said. "There's nothing like a little deprivation to loosen a spoiled kid's tongue. I'll let you know when Luca gives it up."

"You mean if he gives it up."

Nick smiled. "No, I meant when," he said. "Talk to you later."

"Where you headed?"

"Recon. I've got an idea about where we can do the swap."

"Nick?" Max said. "Thanks for everything,"

"Save it for when we've got your boy back," Nick said. He turned away and started west along Beaver Street toward Broadway, looking for a cab.

❖❖❖

"Luca?" the Beak said.

"I have your son," Max said.

A sudden dead silence filled the cyberspace between them.

"Did you hear me?" Max asked. "This is Max Christian, and I said I have your son."

"Impossible," the Beak said. "You're lying."

"You think? Then how is it I'm calling you on Luca's phone?"

"It's a trick. My best men are with him in shifts around the clock. They're under oath to die before they'd let him be taken."

Max snorted. "Turns out your best men either aren't all that good or all that dedicated," he said. "If you really think I'm lying, check your email. You'll find a video made by an associate of mine less than one hour ago. It should be adequate proof both of life and of Luca's present circumstances as—how

145

did you put it?—my guest. Take a look, and call me back. On this phone."

Max rang off and forced a smile of hope toward Meridew and Ahab, who were sitting on his office couch. Hope was a long way from what he was really feeling; he wondered whether any of them could ever feel safe again, even if the exchange came off.

"What did he say?" Meridew asked. "Will he do it? Will he give us Jay back?"

"He doesn't want to believe me," Max said. "He will when he sees the video and hears what else we've got. He'll do it because he has to do it."

The ringtone on Luca's phone sounded, a snippet of Sinatra claiming he'd been a puppet, a pauper, a pirate, a poet, a pawn, and a king. *Yeah right*, Max thought, picking up the call.

"Yo," he said. "Talk to me."

"You've got my son bound and gagged in what looks like a dungeon," the Beak said. "Was that necessary?"

"Sorry about that," Max said. "Your boy exhibited a bit of an attitude, and we were fresh out of bullet ants to correct it. What's your answer—yes or no?"

"I'll do the exchange," the Beak said. "On my terms."

"You don't get to set terms. I do. As you once said to me, I hold all the cards."

"I don't think so," the Beak said.

"You will when you hear what else I've got. Remember that nasty RICO case hanging over your head?"

The Beak laughed. "That?" he said. "It's falling apart."

"That's what you thought when you put the government's star witness in the ground, but I can bring it magically back to life with what I've got. Your beloved son was foolish enough to commit the family secrets to a single thumb drive—which, by the way, is in a safe-deposit box in one of seven hundred ninety-four Chase bank locations in New York, in case you're thinking of trying to get it back. I'm working from one of a dozen extant copies. My associates know what to do with the others if anything unpleasant should happen to me or anyone close to me."

A long moment slid by.

"What have you got?" the Beak said. "Or, rather, what do think you've got, other than the business records of a wholly legitimate corporation?"

"I've got pretty much everything Uncle would need to put you and Luca both in supermax for the rest of your natural lives—your suppliers in Mexico and Colombia, your shipping routes, your distribution network in the States, your unreported income, your money launderers, your payoffs to governments and law enforcement in eight countries. You name it; I've got it, and I'm not halfway into what's here."

"You're lying."

"Gotta say this for your boy's management practices, though—he kept meticulous records," Max said. "My guess is, if that's what they taught him at b-school, they didn't have a criminal conspiracy in mind."

"I repeat: you're lying. Luca is young in the family business, but he isn't stupid."

"That's what I thought until I started reading what's on this drive," Max said. "I guess he figured, hey, he password-protected the bad stuff; it's safe. And it was—until he gave up the password."

"Under coercion, no doubt," the Beak said. "I imagine that in your years in law enforcement, you became familiar with the rule excluding 'the fruit of the poisonous tree' from evidence? I believe that would mean your stolen drive and your coerced password would never see the light of day."

"Unless there's evidence that they were legally obtained. Several witnesses are prepared to testify that that was the case. I'm one of them."

"Perjury is a crime."

"If it can be proven. It'd be my word against Luca's. The NYPD legend against the Paolucci family consigliere, and the legend has two eyewitnesses to back him up. Guess who wins."

The call went silent again.

"Tell me, Don Carlo—you ever done time?"

"Never," the Beak said.

"Neither has Luca, and you need to think what it'll be like for him inside. Fresh meat, handsome kid, twenty-eight and looks younger, and never been in the system? That's called cherry, and there'll be guys in there—big guys muscled up in the yard—who can't wait to pop it."

"No one would touch a don's son. You're bluffing, Detective. Why should I believe you about any of this?"

"You'd best believe me," Max said. "I've even got your hit list, past, present, and future. Your boy wasn't dumb enough to call it that—it's in a folder called 'Contracts,' but it's pretty obvious what it is. There's some interesting names there too. One of your rival dons, Giuseppe Gargano, a.k.a. Joey Lips— he's marked as pending. Two capos from other families are pending. Two or three Gargano soldiers are listed as expired. Couple more are pending, and those are just guys whose names I remembered from my cop days. Oh, and here's one straight out of this week's headlines: I. M. Trubble—expired. The star prosecution witness in your RICO case. Sounds like a hit list to me. You agree?"

"You have an impressive imagination, Detective," the Beak said. "Have you considered a career writing crime fiction?"

"Sorry. I guess I'm still a cop at heart. I prefer fact. And you know who else's names I found on that list? Mine. My wife's. My son's. My partner's. All marked as pending. You can understand I might take that personally."

"This so-called hit list would never stand up as evidence."

"That would be for a judge to decide. But what if it were to mysteriously surface in the *Post*, say, or the *News*? The other four borgatas would be popping caps in your guido ass before the federales got through reading everything I'd given them."

Max could hear whispers at the Beak's end of the call. A minute crawled by and then another.

"You there?" Max asked.

"On advice of counsel," the Beak said, "I will continue this negotiation only if you agree to hand over that thumb drive to me."

"And give up my life insurance? That's a nonstarter, and you know it. The deal is your son for my son—period. The drive stays in preventive detention."

There was another pause. Max heard more whispers and a longer silence. He waited. He could feel beads of sweat forming on his forehead.

"You there?" he asked.

"Tell me your terms," the Beak said. The bravado was gone from his voice.

"We'll do the exchange at ten o'clock Saturday, the day after tomorrow, at a neutral place to be determined. An associate of mine is scouting locations as we speak. We'll each be permitted one soldier and one only. Mine will be my partner, Ahab. I assume yours will be Il Lupo, right?"

"Right. Obviously. And?"

"We'll stand twenty yards apart. Our sons will be released simultaneously. When both are safely with their fathers, we stand down and go our separate ways. Agreed?"

"Agreed," he said.

"Oh," Max said, "and one more thing. My wife would like her money back. All of it, which comes to twenty-two and a half million to date." Max winked at Meridew. "And to show she's not being greedy, she plans to sign over all of it to charity. Agreed?"

This time, the Beak paused. An empty minute slid by; the Beak evidently was measuring the value of his son's life against an eight-figure drain on his treasury.

"Agreed," he said finally.

"Thank you for your cooperative attitude," Max said.

"You're a dead man," the Beak said.

"Maybe," Max said. "But I'll die knowing you'll soon be alone in a cage wishing you were dead too."

CHAPTER 15

By Any Means Necessary

Friday was to have been his day of peace, the lull between the storms of battle, and Max wasn't ready to let go of it when the Sam Cooke ringtone on his BlackBerry sounded at six thirty Saturday morning. His head hurt. His breath was rank. His tongue felt as if it were coated with Astroturf. His whole being wanted it to still be Friday. He couldn't remember where a whole day had gone, and what he critically needed was more sleep.

But Cooke kept insistently singing that a change was gonna come, until Max finally reached for his phone and growled, "Yo, it's the middle of the night. What the fuck?"

"Max?" Nick's voice said. "This is your wake-up call. It's showtime. You need to get your ass in gear and get up to the site."

"I'm on it," Max said. His voice was hoarse.

"You sound like shit."

"I told you I'm good. I'll be there."

"It's your big day. You sure you're in shape to get your butt up here?"

"I will be," Max mumbled without much conviction. "Anyway, Ahab's driving. Best wheelman in the NYPD back when he was on the job. What he says, anyway."

"And he knows where he's going?"

"Yeah, he knows where we're going and how we get there. We went over it yesterday."

The site Nick had scouted for the hostage exchange was a clearing in the woods just beyond Purchase, an enclave for real and aspirational multimillionaires in the Westchester County exurbs.

"Let me guess," Max said. "You're already there."

"Dani and me've been here all night," Nick said.

"Recon?"

"Recon. Special-ops rules—sleep when you've got time; don't when you don't. We've been scouting the woods with night-vision goggles, making sure there's no funny stuff going on. Old rule of my own: always be the first one to the party. I've told you before: I don't like surprises."

"Neither do I. You see anything?"

"I think General Beak's troops are maybe afraid of the dark. I was expecting at least a squad, maybe a platoon, but all we saw was one guy wandering around carrying a MAC-11 in one hand and slapping mosquitoes with the other. He looked like he'd rather be anywhere else."

"And?"

"He got his wish. Dani dealt with him."

"Sent him on vacation?"

"Sent him on vacation," Nick said, "and he's not expected back anytime soon. I told you the girl was tough."

"Like her godfather?"

"Like her father. If you think I'm a warrior, you should've seen Eddie. He got every decoration there is except the Medal of Honor. Which, by the way, he deserved."

Neither man spoke for a long moment.

"So now what?" Max asked, breaking the silence.

"Dani and I'll keep patrolling, 'cause we're expecting more company for sure. My guess? The Beak wouldn't even take a leak with less than two guys guarding the bathroom door. What you need to do meanwhile is get your shit together, hook up with Ahab, and be at the place we talked about by oh-nine-fifteen hours. Gus'll meet you there and get you guys and the package to the site."

"Done," Max said.

"You won't see me there till after," Nick said. "But I'll be there, and I'll have your backs. We set?"

"We're good."

"And be careful getting there. The Beak'll have a lot of soldiers in the street, hoping you'll lead them to the package. They've probably got your house staked out right now. Take evasive action—you think you're up to it?"

"I'll be okay," Max said, "soon as I get a cup of coffee in my belly. I'll see you up there."

"Later," Nick said. "Good luck."

"Hope so," Max said, ringing off. When he got his feet on the floor and his eyes in focus, he saw Meridew walking into the bedroom with what looked like a triple espresso.

"I figured you might need this," she said. "You had a lot to drink yesterday."

"Needed to," he said, taking a grateful first swallow.

"Scared about today?" she said.

"Course I'm scared," he said. "You know how that goes—you were married to a cop once."

"I still am," she said.

"So you know that every cop's mission when he leaves home for roll call in the morning," he said, "is to protect, serve, and get home to his family alive when his tour's done. You can leave the job, but that part of the job never leaves you." He sipped his coffee. "So *yeah*, I drank a lot. I was quieting my nerves."

"And your conscience?" she asked.

"And my conscience," he said. "What are you doing up and dressed this early?"

"I couldn't sleep," she said. "Was that Nick on the phone just now?"

"Yeah," he said. "It's on. I've gotta be out of here in like twenty minutes."

"I'm going with you," she said.

152

Her words brought Max fully awake. "Dew, babe, you can't," he said. "It's too dangerous."

"I don't care," she said. "It's our son—my son—we're talking about. I have to be there for him."

"Babe, please, no," he said. "I'm begging you. Think about it. Let's say the Beak keeps his word and goes through with the exchange, Jay for Luca, okay? He'll send his troops after us when it's done. It'll be even odds whether any of us make it back to the city alive."

"Then I'll die with you and Jay," she said. "What kind of life would I have left without my boys?"

"Babe," he said, "what you're asking—I can't—"

He walked away from her, carrying his coffee into the living room. The curtains were drawn. He parted them just enough for a peek outside. A black Benz SUV was double-parked on the far side of Eighteenth Street. Max could see two men in the front seat. A third stood leaning on the rear door, studiously filing his nails.

"They're already here," Max said, returning to the bedroom. "Three guys I can see, maybe a fourth in their car. My guess is the Beak's hoping I lead them to Luca, so they can snatch him back before we ever get to the site. If they do that, we all die—Jay, you, me, Ahab. I can't let you come, babe. Please."

"I'll take that chance," Meridew said. "I have to be there."

Max sat down beside her on her side of the bed and took her hand. He needed to think, but the clock was running, which meant he had to think fast.

"Okay, babe," he said, "there's maybe a way. You can't be at the site—those ground rules are set in stone. Understood? It's me and Ahab—period."

Meridew nodded.

"You're gonna be watched, okay? What I need you to do is leave here in about an hour, and take a cab to Grand Central, okay? Buy a ticket—where to doesn't matter. Browse the shops, check out the food market, buy a couple of things— you're killing time till your train, okay?"

"Okay so far. And then?"

"Go sit at the Cipriani bar like you're waiting for it to

open. Get busy with your phone as if you're texting friends, okay? Only you're really buzzing Uber to pick you up at the Vanderbilt Avenue exit. You still with me?"

"So far."

"Good, 'cause you're now about to lose anybody still tailing you. Leave your packages like you're coming right back, just stepping outside for a breath of air or a smoke, okay? But you're not coming back—you're hopping into the Uber car, and you're telling the driver, 'Take me to the New Rochelle Municipal Marina.' Repeat that to me."

"The New Rochelle Municipal Marina. I'm not a special-needs child, Max, okay? But won't they follow me?"

"They'll try, but by the time whoever's following you catches on and gets back to his car, you're gone. You get to the marina and wait. We'll bring Jay there."

"Wait how long?"

"That I can't tell you. We're gonna be tailed—that's pretty much a given. Which means we won't be coming by the most direct route. Could be fifteen or twenty minutes. Could be forty-five, depending."

Meridew sat silently, considering her options.

"Look, babe," Max said, "I've gotta get dressed and get going. Let me know, okay?"

"I'll do it," she said. "Your way."

Max hugged her and motored toward the bathroom for what she'd once dubbed, with only slight exaggeration, his two-minute toilette. Actually, it took him eight minutes for a quick spritz in the shower, a once-over-lightly shave, two swipes of Axe, a swish of Listerine, a fistful of Tic Tacs, and the usual struggle to water-comb his untamable hair. When he emerged, he took two more minutes to get into his work clothes: an open shirt, a recently pressed pair of jeans, a blue Lands' End blazer, and his battered And1 gym shoes.

"Come here," Meridew said. She attacked a food stain on his left lapel with a spit-moistened hankie.

"How do I look?" he asked.

"Presentable," she said, "which is where you've set the bar

as long as I've known you. Let's say I didn't marry you for your wardrobe. In fact, I consider you lucky."

"Lucky? How?"

"Lucky that you have no vanity. The more important question is how you feel."

"You mean apart from scared today will go sideways on us? I feel guilty. I mean, I know all rules are suspended when we're talking about our son's life, but I've spent the past few days being party to stuff I used to lock people up for—armed robbery, kidnapping, blackmail, extortion, and, I suspect, accessory to several murders."

"Love, we've had this conversation before," Meridew said. "We asked ourselves if breaking the rules matters with our son's life at stake, and we agreed it doesn't."

"I know, I know, babe," Max said. "It's just—I don't know. I guess I envy Nick. For him, it's all do what needs to be done—period. I mean, I really like the guy, and he sure as hell knows how to get where we want to go, but I'm just not all the way there yet. I'm doing things I don't feel right doing."

"That's not surprising, love. He was a soldier; you were a cop. You had rules; you had boundaries. There are no rules in a war, and boundaries only exist to be defended or breached."

"And we're in a war," Max said. "No, you're right, babe. I've gotta keep reminding myself it is a war, and I've gotta fight it."

"By any means necessary?"

"By any means necessary. See you when the war's over and we've got Jay."

I hope, he added to himself. He wasn't nearly as certain as he'd tried to sound.

There was a damp spring mist in the air, undecided as to whether or not to turn into rain. The Beak's hoods were still at their posts, so Max once again chose the route he'd named after a time-honored basketball maneuver: the backdoor play.

He slipped out a back window and scaled the fire escape, pausing to wave at the two young hospital residents playing hearts in the top-floor apartment. They smiled and waved back.

He low-walked across the rooftops of the brownstones and redbrick low-rises between his town house and the high-rise on the corner.

He descended into the garden of the middle-aged flower children at the far end of the block, taking care not to disturb their daily breakfast of hash brownies and chai. He exchanged peace signs with them, declined their offer of a brownie, and walked through their trustfully unlocked apartment to the street.

He glanced back up the block toward his place. The Beak's boys hadn't budged, so he walked uptown to the 6 train subway stop at Twenty-Second and Lexington. He positioned himself at the downtown end of the platform, where he could spot anyone following him. He saw no one, but he let one train go by and slipped onto the next bare seconds before the doors slid shut behind him.

He got out at Sixty-Eighth Street, losing himself in the perpetual swirl of Hunter College students arriving for class or leaving for home, work, a tryst, or maybe just latte macchiatos at a Starbucks somewhere in the five boroughs. He walked up Lex and across Seventy-First to an unstarred, low-buck coffeehouse where Ahab had staked out a postage-stamp-sized table.

"We got time for a quickie?" Max asked.

"Yeah, if it's really quick," Ahab said. "Clock's ticking."

He got up, ordered at the counter, and walked two double espressos back to the table.

"Bad night, boss?" Ahab asked.

Max nodded.

"Stage fright?"

"Yeah, partly that, I guess, plus a hangover," Max said. He took a healthy swallow of coffee. It burned his tongue but felt good going down. "You come heavy?" he asked.

"Yeah, my Ruger," Ahab said, "plus a forty-five case somebody comes at us hard and needs stopping. You?"

"Just my SIG. Lot of old guys on the job talk about how

semiautos can jam on you, but mine's kept me alive—till now anyway." He drained the last of his coffee and set the cup down. "You scared?" he asked.

"I don't think so," Ahab said.

"I am, a little bit," Max said. "I won't get that adrenaline rush till we're there."

"Funny thing," Ahab said. "I never think about getting dead."

"You don't have a family," Max said. "I do—up to today anyway. Let's go."

They walked around the block to a Chrysler 300 Ahab had rented the night before. "Like it, boss?" he said.

"You had to go premium, didn't you?" Max said. "Like Christian Enquiries has been raking in the bucks since this whole thing with Jay went down."

"Forgive me, boss, but I felt a need for speed. I've been tailed since I picked this baby up. Real cute too—they're running relays so I don't get used to seeing one car on my black ass all the way."

"Pretty smart. I wonder if it was Beaky's idea or Luca's—part of the new cutting-edge, next-gen corporate paradigm."

"But not smart enough for your partner," Ahab said, smiling. "They're too obvious. See the maroon Buick double-parked outside the CVS back at the corner, like somebody just ducked in to pick up a Viagra refill or something?"

"Yeah, I see him," he said.

"That's our new best friend," Ahab said. "He just subbed in for a black Caddy that looked like a stray from a funeral procession. The Caddy subbed in for a Cherokee—you get the picture."

"Well, smart guy, you been away from the car any length of time?"

"Only just now," Ahab said. "For, what, ten or twelve minutes?"

"Long enough for the guy in the Caddy to plant a tracker," Max said. "Let's have a look."

They took opposite sides of the car and did a quick check of the places where hidden GPS trackers worked best: the bumpers, fenders, gas tank, and near undersides of the chassis.

"Look what I found, boss," Ahab said, rising from a squat on the street side. He was holding a tracker not much larger than a pack of cigarettes.

"Toss it," Max said.

"He'll see us."

"So what? All it'll tell him is he needs to stick a little closer to us to earn his pay. Gives us better eyes on him."

They got in the Chrysler, pulled away from the curb, rounded the corner, and headed west toward Third Avenue. As Max had guessed, the maroon Buick was a bare few yards behind their back bumper.

"Wouldn't we have done better taking the FDR Drive 'stead of Third?" Max asked as they turned uptown. "We'd get there faster."

"Chill, boss," Ahab said. "We'll be on time. I just want to shake our traveling companion first."

"You think you can? The Beak's got guys who do this for a living."

"Watch me. Oh, and please be sure your seat belt is securely fastened and your tray table is in an upright position, 'cause this could be a seriously bumpy ride."

They cruised into the Nineties with the Beak's man still close behind. At Ninety-Sixth, Ahab slowed and paused at a yellow light.

The light turned red.

"Hold tight, boss," Ahab said. He mashed the accelerator to the floor, hung a wide right across three lanes of traffic, and somehow slipped through a fleeting opening in the two-way flow on Ninety-Sixth.

"Jesus, Ahab!" Max yelped, bracing both hands against the dashboard.

There was a loud double crunch of metal on metal behind

them. Max glanced at the rearview mirror. From what he could tell, the goombah in the maroon Buick had tried to match Ahab's maneuver and had, as the saying went, run shit out of luck. An eastbound U-Haul truck had T-boned him on one side. A westbound SUV had T-boned him on the other. What remained of the Buick was a blob of steel, chrome, and glass in a funhouse-mirror likeness of a figure eight. Smoke was belching out from under the hood. The car alarm was sounding. There was blood on what was left of the windshield.

"We've gotta stop," Max said.

"Why?" Ahab asked.

"We're leaving the scene of a fucking accident is why. That's fifteen years if the guy's dead, which it looks like he could be."

Ahab shrugged. "Wasn't our accident," he said. "Was his accident."

"But we caused it," Max said.

"Naw, boss, he caused it, making a turn like that. If we were still cops, we'd be cuffing that hump for reckless endangerment one." He eased the Chrysler onto I-87 and sped north toward Westchester County. "Plus which," he said, smiling, "I heard we got someplace to be."

CHAPTER 16

In the Clearing

They walked into Boiano Bakery in Mamaroneck and saw Nick's pal Gus sitting alone at a table, drumming the tabletop with the two surviving fingers on his left hand. Three espressos in paper cups and a plate of biscotti were arrayed before him. His cup was empty. The others were full but had given up steaming.

"You guys are late," he said.

"What, by two or three minutes?" Max asked.

"You'd ever been in a combat zone, you'd know oh-nine-fifteen means oh-nine-fifteen, not oh-nine-eighteen," Gus said. "I ordered you coffee for oh-nine-fifteen. You got two minutes to drink it or not and grab a couple biscotti for the road 'cause we're moving outa here at oh-nine-twenty."

The espresso had gone cold. Ahab took a pass, but Max downed his, hoping to chase the last of the cobwebs enveloping his brain. He'd skipped breakfast, so he stuffed a fistful of biscotti into a blazer pocket.

"Where's the package?" he asked.

"In the van," Gus said. "Wrapped tight and resting, last I checked. Boy didn't enjoy his boat trip all that much." He glanced at his watch. "If you guys are done," he said, "we need to move on out."

160

They crossed Mamaroneck Avenue to the gray Bug Brothers van nested where Gus had parked it. "Ahab, leave your car here; you're riding shotgun with me," Gus said. "Max, the bad guys know you; you need to be out of sight. You're in back, keeping the package company."

"He behaving himself?" Max asked.

"Now, yeah," Gus said. "He was copping an attitude this morning, so I stirred maybe half a dozen crushed Xanax into his breakfast feed at oh-five-thirty. Quieted him right down. There's some more of them babies back there, if he acts up again."

"Or I can just duct-tape his mouth," Max said. "Variant on Occam's razor—the simplest silencer is the best."

"Yeah, well," Gus said. "Let's move."

Max hoisted himself into the back of the van and heard Gus locking the door behind him. In the dim interior light, he saw Luca sitting with his hands cuffed behind him and his ankles bound with clothesline. His eyes were watery. His clothes stank of sweat and urine. His Gekko coif was in an advanced state of disarray. His mind was where Max's had been that morning: groping for coherence. He looked at Max with dull, heavy-lidded eyes.

"You!" he said.

"Me," Max said, easing to a seat opposite Luca on the van floor. "Your best friend right now, taking you back to your daddy. Are you gonna be a well-behaved boy, or are you gonna make me put you back to sleep? I've got some more of that magic potion if you want. Or I've got a nearly whole roll of duct tape in case you prefer that. It's your day, so it's your call."

"Fuck you," Luca said. His voice was low, and his speech was slurred.

"I don't call that well behaved. I might have to make an addition to the menu and wash your mouth out with soap instead."

Luca stared balefully at Max. His morning's Xanax cocktail

was wearing off fast, giving way to a rising anger that flashed in his eyes and sharpened his speech.

"Fuck you twice, along with that faggoty son of yours," he said. "I hope you both have a nice day. It'll be your last."

Max laughed. "I'd have thought your daddy would be more disciplined than that—especially with all that documentary evidence you were kind enough to gift me with. It's more than enough to put you and Daddy both in supermax for life if anything happens to me or my family."

"Oh, my father is definitely a disciplined man—he never acts out of anger. He never even carries a weapon. Il Lupo is another matter."

"Il Lupo acts on your father's orders."

"Usually, not always. He's a feral beast—a wolf, as his name suggests. Wolves are not house pets. They don't sit or roll over and play dead on command. They can't be reliably tamed."

"I've alerted your father to the stakes in this game. He strikes me as a man who takes consequences into account."

"True," Luca said, "but Il Lupo is a pure man of action. He lives solely in the moment. Consequences have no meaning for him. Neither does conscience."

"In this situation," Max said, "it won't matter whether he acts on orders or on impulse. The consequences for you and your father will be the same if any harm comes to me or my son, so you might as well just shut the fuck up with your threats and go back to sleep."

Max's drugstore Timex claimed the ride took just eighteen minutes, but time being subjective, it felt to him more like three hours; when they finally got where they were going, his tailbone was sore from jouncing on the van's corrugated steel floor. When the door finally swung open, he squinted into the sudden sunlight and found himself at the edge of a thickly wooded area just beyond the villas and mansions of Purchase. Max unlocked Luca's wrists, untethered his ankles, heaved him to his feet, and handed him down to Gus more gently than he deserved.

"Courtesy of UPS," he said. "Handle with care, Gus—the boy's still kinda wobbly. You sure that wasn't smack you put in his IV breakfast this morning?"

"Nah," Gus said, "he's just got landlubber syndrome. Spends, what, forty-four hours on a moored boat on quiet waters and acts like he just missed the last lifeboat off the *Titanic*. He'll be okay; he's just a baby is all." He slapped Luca sharply, once on each cheek, to quicken his wake-up and lowered him to a seat in the one-lane gravel roadway. "He better be okay—it's a klick and change from here to the site, and it's not like a stroll down Fifth Avenue. It's all woods."

"So how do we get there?"

"Walk."

"I get that," Max said. "Which way?"

Gus waved Max and Ahab to the edge of the woods, out of earshot for Luca.

"Dani—remember her?" Gus said. "She marked out a path for you. See the strip of yellow packing tape on that birch over here?"

"I'm pavement raised," Max said. "I don't know a birch from a Christmas tree. But yeah, I see the tape on a tree."

"Okay, start there," Gus said, "and look for markers like that every ten or so meters. You'll know the site when you get there. You hearing me?"

"We're hearing you," Max said. "Follow the yellow tape road, right?"

"Right, only on your way back, peel the tape. Get me? Anybody's trying to follow you, you don't want to make it easy for 'em, right? I'm gonna be waiting right here for you, and anybody comes out of those woods, I'd rather it's you two guys and the kid than Charlie Beak's crew, okay?"

"Okay," Max said. "We better get started."

"Yeah, but before you go, I got something for you boys," Gus said. He led Max and Ahab back to the van, rummaged in a rucksack stashed behind the driver's seat, and emerged with two Kevlar ballistic vests, one in each hand. "Put these on," he said. "They're pretty light—light for body armor anyway. They'll fit under your jackets."

"What about him?" Max whispered, pointing toward Luca with one discreet thumb.

"Him?" Gus said loudly enough for Luca to hear. "Silly me. I musta forgot. I didn't bring but the two. Looks like pretty boy'll just have to take his chances if the lead starts flying."

Max and Ahab shucked their jackets long enough to wriggle into their vests.

"Fucks up my line," Ahab said, his slim-cut suit coat back in place.

"Fuck your line," Max said. "Let's get the package and start walking. Front-and-follow?"

"Yeah," Ahab said, "but I got front. I don't want you first out of the forest if Mr. Beak and his boys are planning the wrong kind of welcoming party. It'll be you they're gunning for, not me."

Finding their way through the woods was easy, thanks to Dani's trail markers, but Luca slowed their progress by finding inventive ways to make himself burdensome. His legs were still rubbery after his time trussed up belowdecks on Gus's boat. He complained loudly about the mosquitoes attacking his arms, the pollen making him sneeze, and the soft earth taking the last shine off his Bruno Magli bit loafers. At one point, he sat down on the forest floor and burst into tears.

"What the fuck is it now?" Max demanded.

"Look at this," he sobbed. A tick had attached itself to his left ankle and was contentedly battening on his blood. "Like this whole thing isn't nightmare enough," he wailed. "Now I'm gonna get Lyme disease out of it."

Max drew his SIG, leveled it at a point between Luca's eyes, and chambered a round. "Look, babycakes, your odds of getting Lyme disease from one tick are like a gazillion to one. That's for openers, okay? You've got two choices here. One, quit blubbering, get moving, and let your nice daddy take care of your little booboo—maybe one of his goons is packing a pair of tweezers and a Mickey Mouse Band-Aid. Two, we can take you back to the boat for an IV lunch, and you can forget about going home. There are no other options, and you're taking time off the clock."

"Fuck you," Luca grumbled, but he managed to get back on his feet.

"No, fuck you, Little Lord Fauntleroy," Max said, "and I'd strongly advise you to get walking and keep your yap shut. You feel me? I've got people in the woods, and my guess is your daddy does too. You keep noising off, you could get us caught in a blind crossfire, and we're all dead, even precious little new-paradigm you. Understood?"

Luca's response was a pouty frown. His lower lip poked out almost far enough to cast a shadow. But he fell in behind Ahab and resumed the trek, his complaints reduced to a steady, monotonic mumble: "I'm not used to this. Pop, send someone. Help me. Now I'm sweating. I'm getting a fever. It's prob'ly Lyme. I need a doctor. What if I fucking go into a coma before we even get there? Where're Lupo's men? What are we paying them for anyway? I'm dying over here. I'm on fire. I should be in the hospital. Help me, somebody. Please help. Please. Please ..."

"Can I get some cheese with that whine?" Max asked finally, his voice ominously low.

Luca glared at him, but the flow of grievances stopped.

They came to the end of the trail, and Max stepped out alone into the bright May sunlight, leaving Luca in Ahab's irritable care. It was 10:02 by Max's Timex, which made him at least arguably on time. He saw Charlie Beak and Il Lupo standing together toward the far end of a grassy clearing maybe half the size of a football field. Jay was out of sight and, Max guessed, under guard beyond the tree line—if he was really there at all.

Max walked toward the Beak with his left hand in the air

as a gesture of peace and his right at his side, holding his SIG, as a deterrent to war. Il Lupo raised his shotgun to waist level, but at a whispered word from his boss, he lowered it and took the threat level down to a homicidal glare.

The Beak stepped forward alone, extending a hand. Max ignored it.

"You're looking sharp, Signore Paolucci," he said, sizing up the Beak's tailored gray-on-gray pinstripes and high-gloss, pointy-toed shoes. "Dinner at Patsy's later? Rao's maybe? Celebrating the safe return of your son and heir?"

"I dress as I normally dress, Detective," the Beak said, "and I had the benefit of a cleared pathway to this open space. You, evidently, have not. You look as if you'd spent the night in the woods and slept in your clothes—or did you just come here in your normal dress-down Friday attire?"

"These are my work clothes," Max said. "Your trade no doubt requires you to look important. Mine doesn't. Shall we skip the small talk and get on with it?"

"By all means," the Beak said. "But where is my son?"

"In the care of my partner, in the woods," Max said. "Where's my son?"

"At a turn in the pathway, just out of sight from where we're standing," the Beak said. "He has been rather subdued since his encounter with the bullet ants, but I can assure you his stay with me has caused him no lasting harm of any consequence."

"Let me see him," Max said.

"When I've seen my son," the Beak said, "and have reassured myself that he has not been mistreated by you and your henchmen."

"I'm afraid he's not had the creature comforts you've spoiled him with," Max said. "To put it bluntly, his behavior has been pretty fucking tiresome. We had to keep him confined by himself as a matter of self-defense against his constant whining. But you have my word there's not a mark on him."

"Neither is there a mark on your boy, Detective," the Beak said. "You're aware of the disciplinary measures I've had to impose when he—or, in one instance, you—misbehaved. They caused him no lasting harm, I assure you."

"So?" Max said.

"So," the Beak said.

The two stood face-to-face two feet apart in a silent stare-down. A minute passed, then another.

"Look," Max said finally, "we can stand here eye-fucking each other, or we can get this thing moving. Let's get out our phones and, on a count of three, tell our people to bring our—"

"Our guests?"

"*POWs* is the term I was reaching for."

"*POW* belongs to the vocabulary of war," the Beak said. "I thought we had arrived at a cease-fire, at least for today."

"A cease-fire implies mutual trust, and you haven't earned mine. To resume, on three, we bring our POWs forward. Agreed?"

"Agreed."

"One more thing, though," Max said. "I wonder if you've noticed that a number of your employees have gone off on unscheduled vacations in the past couple of weeks."

"I have indeed noticed," the Beak said. "I suppose I have you to thank?"

"My associates, actually. They're less burdened by moral ambiguity than I am."

"And you're telling me this now because?"

"I thought it would be only fair to let you know that several more of your soldiers have gone AWOL during the night," Max said. "I mean, in case you wondered why you hadn't earned my trust. Shall we make our calls?"

Hate burned in the Beak's eyes, but on Max's count of three, both men jabbed at their smartphones and told their men to bring the hostages to their assigned spots in the clearing.

To his rear, Max heard the last crunch of dry leaves underfoot as Ahab marched Luca out of the woods. Straight ahead, he saw Jay emerge on the far edge of the clearing, flanked by two of the Beak's hoods.

"Lupo, take these punks out!" Luca shouted into the stillness. "That's an order! Clip them now!"

Once again, Il Lupo raised his shotgun to waist level.

The Beak pushed it downward with the flat of his palm and took a step in Max's direction. "If you're ready," he called, "let us proceed. My men have marked off our respective positions with stripes of white field-marking paint precisely twenty yards apart, as we agreed."

Max felt a sudden chill as he walked with Ahab and Luca to their appointed spots in the clearing. What had the Beak whispered to Il Lupo? It could have been the weather or the time of day. It could have been a reminder of what was at stake if anybody got hurt. Or it could have been something closer to Max's best guess: "Not now, Lupo. Later. Wait till we've got Luca back. Then whack them all. The father. The son. And that unholy spook they've got with them."

CHAPTER 17

The Massacre in the Woods

The chill sharpened when Max got his first good look at his son across the no-man's-land between the two parties to the exchange. Jay's face was ashy pale. His head was bowed, and his shoulders were slumped—the posture of a political prisoner leaving a reeducation camp. He'd lost some weight in captivity and, from what Max could see of his arms, some muscle tone as well. He was wearing the orange jumper chosen for him by the Student of Pain. When he finally looked up, he smiled faintly and mouthed the word *Dad*. But his eyes were distant and unrevealing, like windows with their shades three-quarters drawn.

"Your son's a pussy," Luca whispered into Max's ear. "My pop treated him far better than you and your creepy friends treated me."

"That's pretty fucking funny," Max whispered back, "coming from someone who was on the ground bawling like a baby ten minutes ago 'cause he had a tick stuck to his leg. One tick versus twenty-five bullet ants, and *you're* calling *my* son a pussy?"

Across the divide, the Beak raised a hand and beckoned Max to meet him at the halfway point between them. "If you and my son have finished what appears to be a pleasant parting chat, Detective," he said, "might I suggest that we go forward with what we've met here to do this morning?"

Max nodded.

"Good," the Beak said. "And might I further suggest that, once again on a count of three, our sons step forward unaccompanied and start walking to their fathers?"

"Works for me," Max said.

"I further propose that both you and your partner keep your weapons holstered during the course of the exchange. Il Lupo is under orders to hold his shotgun pointed at the ground with his finger outside the trigger housing. I, as always, have come unarmed."

"How brave," Max said.

"It's not bravery, Detective—unlike the other dons of the Five Families, I am quite unafraid of dying. I look to our Lord and Savior as my ultimate protector. You, of course, wouldn't understand that, being Christian in name only."

"Oh, I understand," Max said. "But I also am aware that you haven't placed your safety solely in God's hands. You have, what, fifty button men? A hundred?"

The Beak smiled. "Oh, more than that. You'd have to ask Luca in your few moments left with him. Our human resources department would have the exact count, and they report to him, not me. But you're quite right that a man in my position cannot be shielded by faith alone."

"So let me guess—your HR department head is Il Lupo."

"Correct. But we're wasting time with chatter. Shall we resume our places and proceed?"

"Let's do it," Max said.

The Beak turned and strode briskly back to his spot, as if he were hosting a Sunday picnic. Max, with less bravura, made his retreat walking backward, his eyes fixed on Il Lupo and his gun hand tightening around the butt of the SIG Sauer on his right hip.

"You scared, Detective?" Luca taunted when they were side by side again. "You should be."

"Shut up and listen, babycakes," Max said. "Your daddy's

going to count to three. You hear *three*, start walking toward his loving arms. You think you can remember all that, genius?"

Luca was fumbling for a snappy response, when they heard the Beak begin the countdown.

"One!"

The sound seemed to echo from the tree line all around them. Across the divide, Jay caught Max's eye and, almost imperceptibly, shook his head.

"Two!"

Max's gaze roamed from Il Lupo back to Jay. Again, he saw the head shake, so subtle it could have been mistaken for a nervous tic. This time, Jay bowed his head and stared down at his own left hand hanging at his side. His thumb pointed for a millisecond toward Il Lupo. His index finger flexed once and then again, as if pulling an invisible trigger.

"Three!"

In the days that followed, the tabloids would call what followed the Massacre in the Woods and would impose a tidy narrative order on it. But for Max, there was only the shapeless disorder called chaos. The two hostages started across the neutral patch of grass, with Luca speed-walking toward his father and Jay veering suddenly into Il Lupo's sight line. Il Lupo's pump-action shotgun was suddenly at shoulder level, and there was the sudden, sharp crack of a rifle from the woods behind them all. Il Lupo dropped suddenly to his knees with blood spreading down his chest from his left shoulder, and his shotgun was suddenly rising again. Max and Ahab fired shot after sudden shot at him until his face was a pulpy red blob, his chest was belching blood, and his massive body lay twitching in the grass, with his longtime padrone, Charlie Beak, standing as still and grave as a tombstone at his side. The intrinsic suddenness of chaos gave way to a still, entropic calm, with Max at its center, watching his son take the first free steps on his journey home.

Jay moved slowly at first, his feet dragging and his head still bowed as if in defeat; at a point, he stumbled, fell to his knees, and seemed to struggle to get upright again. Max rushed to help, half watching a curious scene play out behind them: the Beak greeted Luca with a perfunctory handshake and what looked like an angry scolding. Max couldn't make out the words, but he could almost hear the father's hard forefinger jabs tattooing his son's rib cage.

Then Jay was in his arms. The two of them hugged, laughing and crying at the same time. "Dad, I almost gave up hope," Jay said. "I really thought I'd die in that place. I thought you'd never come. I thought I'd never see you or Mom again."

"I'm crazy sorry, Jaybird. I'm sorry it took me so long. I'm sorry this ever happened. I'm sorry for all of it," Max said. He could taste the salt of Jay's tears mingled with his own. "I blame myself," he said, "but I promised I'd get you back, and here I am, and here you are. You're free."

"They were going to kill us both, Dad—Ahab too. I was standing right there; I heard him say it—the boss, Don Carlo. The fat guy, Il Lupo, wanted to get us all right away, but Don Carlo said, 'No, wait'll we're sure Luca's in the clear. Then clip 'em all. We can't leave any witnesses.' That's why I moved kinda sideways like I did—to get between him and you."

"You risked your life for mine?" Max looked at his son with flooded eyes and gave his shoulder a squeeze. "If this was a real war," he said, "you'd be getting a medal."

Jay managed a first fragile try at a smile. "Not for bravery, Dad," he said. "I've been scared since the moment they grabbed me."

"It's over, Jay. I promise you. You're safe now. We're all safe."

"But won't he try again? Don Carlo? He hates you. He kept saying so the whole time."

"He wouldn't dare come at us unless he's nuts," Max said. "Let's say we've got insurance. One mismove, and he spends the rest of his life in prison. Him and his son."

"For real, Dad?"

"For real, Son."

"And Mom—where's Mom? Is she okay?"

"She's good. She's waiting for us ten or fifteen minutes from here. We'll all go home together," Max said, tightening his embrace. "The important thing is you're safe now. You're with me. You're—"

"Dad, behind you!" Jay cried out. "He's coming!"

Max turned and saw the Beak walking toward them alone. His once immaculate pinstripes were splashed with Il Lupo's blood. His stride was imperious, the straight-backed march of a general unwilling to concede that he'd lost the war.

He was practically chest to chest with Max when he halted. Ahab had dropped to a shooter's crouch. Jay had broken free from his father's arms and skittered inside the tree line, out of sight.

Max signaled Ahab to go be with Jay. He drew his SIG but kept it pressed to his thigh. He felt frozen, paralyzed. His gun hand was unaccountably sweating. A fragment from Yeats was playing in his head: *"The best lack all conviction."* He had convictions, but he had always relied more on instinct, and instinct had deserted him. The Beak was in his face, and he had no idea what he would or ought to do.

"You are most fortunate that I have no weapon," the Beak said. "Your actions today have compounded your debt to me, and you will pay one day—I can assure you of that."

"You kidnapped and tortured my son," Max said, "and I'm in debt to you? Tell me—how's that work?"

"You, sir, are the torturer," the Beak said. "I may have disciplined your son a time or two when his behavior warranted it. But I didn't keep him bound, gagged, and caged in the dark day and night, as you did my son."

"Your son required restraints, Signore Becco, as I've told you," Max said. "He is all attitude all the time, and that scene the two of you played just now tempted me to think you would agree. That wasn't exactly a warm welcome home."

"I am not a sentimentalist, Detective, as you appear to be," the Beak replied. "I have no time for tears. I am a businessman doing business in an uncommonly dangerous world. I cannot afford to be careless, and neither can my son. Had he understood that, you would never have taken him."

"As you just now felt obliged to remind him?"

"For his own good, Detective. I love my son, as you love

yours, but he is not only my son—he is my consigliere and the future don of the Paolucci family. The one sin I cannot forgive him is incaution, and I felt obliged to tell him so. There would be no future for him, for me, or for our borgata if I were to pamper him."

"There'll be no future for either of you if you come at me or my family again. Anything happens to any of us, you and your son will be locked up for life. That's if Joey Lips doesn't get to you first when he sees you've got a contract out on him."

"I am a patient man, Detective," the Beak said. "I have an earned reputation for settling scores. When I settle them is of small concern to me so long as they are settled. It may be a month from now, it may be a year, or it may be a decade, but be assured your day will come. I hope you sleep well in the meantime."

"You too," Max said. "Get your rest now. You won't be sleeping on feather beds where you'll be going."

There was a rustling in the trees behind them, and Nick emerged, barely recognizable in a camouflage suit adorned head to foot with mostly fake foliage. He was carrying a sniper rifle in the crook of his left arm and a Walther PPQ .45 in his right hand. The Walther was pointed at the Beak's breastbone.

"Jesus, Nick," Max said. "You scared the hell out of me in that getup. First glance, I thought you were Bigfoot coming for me."

"This getup," Nick said, "is called a ghillie suit, the latest in high-end sniper wear. Sorry if it frightened you. You wear this, you got cover when you're working in the woods or the tall grass."

"Nice shot, by the way," Max said. "Taking Lupo down like that. I owe you."

"It was you and Ahab put him to sleep," Nick said. "I didn't have a clean shot with your boy in the way."

"You knocked him to his knees," Max said. "Ahab and I just administered the coup de grâce."

The Beak stood watching the exchange in gelid silence, unfazed by the .45 a hand's breadth from his heart; his stare was as blank and his body as still as an effigy's at Madame Tussauds wax museum.

Nick glanced at him. "Max," he growled, "why is this ass-wipe sociopath still alive?"

Max shrugged.

"C'mon, man," Nick said. "Do him. Put him out of his misery."

"I can't," Max said. "Not now."

"You can't?" Nick snapped. "Not now? When're you ever gonna get a better chance?"

"I just can't," Max said. "It's not time."

"You want me to take him out? I'll do him if you don't want to get your hands all bloody."

"No, man, no," Max said. "Give him this moment. This day."

"Why?"

"He's a dad; I'm a dad. I've got my son back; he's got his son back. Let them go home and be together. For today anyway."

"So they can do what—start planning how to do you?"

"If that's what they do, that's what they do. They know the consequences."

"Yeah?" Nick said, his gaze still fixed on the Beak. "So do you. Only if you let them go now, it won't matter. They'll be in jail, but you'll be dead—your family too. Those are your consequences."

Max smiled. "There's an old Rolling Stones song," he said. "'Sympathy for the Devil'—ever heard it?"

Nick shook his head.

"Probably crazy," Max said, "and it's a one-day-only sale, but that's what I think I'm feeling right now—sympathy for the devil."

"Sympathy?" Nick snorted. "Back in Fallujah and Helmand, we used to say *sympathy*'s just a word in the dictionary between *shit* and *syphilis*. You see enough of your buddies blown up by IEDs or kids in suicide vests, *sympathy*'s a word that falls out of your vocabulary real fast."

"I hear you," Max said, "but like I said, now's not the time. Not for me."

They turned toward the Beak, who'd stood watching the debate with a thin, detached smile.

"Look at this guy smirking," Nick said. "He must think we're funny." He pressed his .45 to the bridge of the Beak's prodigious nose. "We funny to you?" he demanded.

"No, not funny," the Beak said. "But amusing as a case study in the folly of sentiment."

"Are you saying you'd kill you if you were me?" Max asked.

"I'd have you killed, yes," the Beak said. "For a student of pain, your ambivalence is itself what poker players call a tell."

"A tell telling you what?"

"Telling me that for all your celebrated heroics as a policeman, you, Detective, are an idealist. A romantic. A man of inaction. A prisoner of ambivalence. I wouldn't need ants or implements to cause you pain. I'd strip naked, give you a gun, and stand before you unarmed, as we find ourselves now. Your fear of doing wrong would be torment enough."

"Fuck off, asshole," Max snapped. "Get the fuck out of here before I change my mind. Go! Now!"

"*Addio, finocchio,*" the Beak said. He flashed a last haughty stare, turned, and walked back to where he'd left Luca. Max watched the two of them cross the clearing toward their pathway through the trees as the father continued his lecture on carelessness; the words were inaudible across the widening distance, but the Beak's rat-a-tat finger jabs to Luca's ribs told the ongoing story.

When they'd disappeared, Nick laid a broad hand on Max's shoulder and gave it a squeeze tight enough to hurt. "Y'know, my friend, I like you, I trust you, and I hope we get to partner up again sometime. But I gotta say, there're times when I don't get you."

"Like just now?" Max asked.

"Like just now. That guy's in your face, threatening you and your whole family, and you've got a chance to drop him on the spot. You're gonna let him walk like that?"

"Like I said, I couldn't drop him. Not today."

"I dunno, Max. In a war, you don't ever give the enemy a second chance. You got him in your sights, there's no such thing as 'not today'—there's only now."

"So you're thinking the Beak was right when he said I was—what was it?—a man of inaction? Scared of doing wrong?"

"That's not what I'm thinking. You didn't go all gooey when we kidnapped his kid. You didn't sweat it when you and Ahab dropped Il Lupo just now. It's letting the Beak off the hook I still don't get. If it was me, I'd have put him down before he ever got this close. Wasn't long ago you yourself were talking the same way."

Max fell silent and looked away. "I guess," he said finally, "it goes back to when my uncle who raised me kept nagging me about why I wanted to be a cop, and I kept saying, 'Justice. I want to serve justice.' Where's the justice in shooting an unarmed man the day he's reunited with his son?"

"I get what you're talking about," Nick said. "But you know what us Sicilians say? We say there's no justice—there's just us."

"I guess I'm still a cop," Max said. "Justice takes time; cops know that. I can wait."

"And I guess I'm still Sicilian," Nick said. "Where my roots are, if you waited for justice, you waited forever. If you wanted justice, you took care of business yourself."

Max shrugged and smiled.

Nick smiled back and wrapped a sinewy arm around Max's shoulders. "Go be with your family," he said. "Gus'll take you guys back to the city on the boat. If I was you, I might be thinking about holing up in a hotel for a few days. Let things quiet down a little, y'know?"

"Nah, we're going home," Max said. "What about you?"

"I've gotta go back and collect Dani. We'll be okay driving back to town—couple of tourists nobody knows."

"Will I see you again?"

"Oh, I'm not leaving right away—I've got a case to close while I'm here. Maybe we can get together for dinner when I'm done. Maybe ask Tina to join us."

"And Dani?" Max said.

"That's a maybe," Nick said. "I'll be dropping her off at LaGuardia so she can get back to Nick & Eddie's. We love our staff, but you leave any restaurant untended more'n a day or two, you can come home to an empty till."

They were shaking hands goodbye, when they heard the report of a rifle shot echo from the woods at the far end of the clearing.

"Speaking of Dani," Nick said. "The girl's as good with one of these M24s as I am." He patted his sniper rifle. "Well, almost as good. I trained her."

"She didn't—"

"Drop Charlie Beak? No, he and his crybaby kid are long gone by now. Probably one of his soldiers wandered into her space. The girl can get kinda grouchy when that happens."

Max laughed. "I thought you two had sent all his boys on vacation by now," he said.

"My guess is whoever caught that bullet was the last one," Nick said. "Except probably whoever's driving the Beak and his boy home. It's a long walk to Rye Brook, and my girl's got *some* mercy in her."

"Thanks again, Nick," Max said. "For everything. Your check will be in the mail soon as I'm home."

"I don't take checks, and I don't do mail. You can bring an envelope to dinner."

"Done," Max said.

"Now, go," Nick said. "Catch up with Ahab and your kid— his mom is waiting. And don't forget to peel the tape off the fucking trees. It's possible we did miss somebody."

CHAPTER 18

Dead Meat

Weekends were always slow in a boutique PI practice like Max's. People of the sort who could afford his thousand-dollar daily fee typically saved their tales of woe till Monday morning, when the martini haze had cleared and the damage they'd done one another on Friday and Saturday nights could be fully assessed; Sundays gave them time to order their thoughts, reassess their differences, and rehearse their lines. So a week to the day after his son's deliverance, Max allowed himself to sleep late and skip even a perfunctory morning shower and shave. It wasn't till he'd pulled on his Wranglers and his faded Penn sweatshirt that he noticed the Next New Girl sprawled facedown on Meridew's side of the bed. Her head was under the pillow, sheltered from the morning light. He pulled the sheet up to cover her naked backside and started downstairs, trying to remember how she'd gotten there.

He remembered Dew having announced at breakfast the day before that she was going back to her dowager mama's house on the Main Line with Jay; he'd need her, she said, as long as it took him to bury his memories of captivity and reintegrate into life at Penn. Max had fallen into a daylong sulk at the news—he recalled that too. He'd had a lot to drink, leaving Ahab to take care of their active cases; he wasn't quite sure when he'd stopped watering his Mount Gay with tonic and started pouring himself straight shots instead. He remembered having wandered out to the reception room and telling the Next New Girl, "Hey, kid, time to go home," to which she'd replied, "Oh, it's okay. I can stay if you want." What had happened next was a blank; there was only the clear circumstantial evidence that she'd visited his bed and the high probability that they'd had sex. If so, he hoped it hadn't been as forgettable for her as it appeared to have been for him; he felt he owed her at least a good time.

Since he couldn't otherwise parse the remains of the night, didn't feel like making breakfast, and felt the throb of a hangover coming on, he declared it a Bloody Mary morning and walked up Third Avenue to the Bluebell Café. An earlier riser had left a copy of the morning's *Post* on the table next to Max's favorite, near the back. The page-one headline screamed for his attention: "DEAD MEAT!" Across the bottom of the page was a streamer: "Mob Big Diced, Sliced, Iced by Killer Fridge."

Max appropriated the paper and flipped to the story, ignoring the Bloody Mary that had appeared at his elbow.

> Mob boss Carlo (Charlie Beak) Paolucci was blown to bits in his posh Midtown tower apartment early today when he opened a refrigerator wired with C-4 plastic explosives.
>
> Crack homicide detective Tina Falcone said the so-called Gentleman Don apparently triggered the violent explosion while raiding the killer fridge for a midnight snack.
>
> One detective at the scene said Paolucci's remains "looked like sliced deli meat." Another said there were "Beakburger makings lying all over the kitchen floor."
>
> The bodies of two Paolucci soldiers were found elsewhere in the apartment, their throats slashed by the intruders. Police said the two

180

had been watching a porn video on the living room TV.

Who planted the explosives was a mystery, but Falcone said the killing had "all the earmarks of a hit by a rival Cosa Nostra family." She said the main focus was on Joseph (Joey Lips) Gargano, whose crew had notoriously tense relations with the Paolucci family.

"We have solid intel that Paolucci had put out a contract on Gargano's life, and Gargano knew it," Falcone said.

She said the fridge bomb was possibly foreshadowed by last week's Massacre in the Woods outside Purchase, New York, in which an apparent Paolucci family conclave was ambushed by unknown assailants.

"Charlie Beak apparently got away at that time," Falcone said, but his chief enforcer, Gianni (The Wolf) Giacalone, and five other soldiers were gunned down.

The coverage ran on for three full tabloid pages, with sidebars on the Beak as ruler of the city's drug trade, the declining fortunes of his rivals among the Five Families in the age of RICO, the rumored anger of the Cosa Nostra's ruling commission over the unsanctioned acts of war among the New York borgatas, and Tina Falcone's previous heroics in closing some of the city's most notorious murder cases. But Max had read all he needed to read. Smiling, he tossed the paper back onto the next table and attacked his cooling bacon and eggs with renewed appetite. His head had cleared. His hangover was gone. The Bloody Mary stood untouched, an orphan no longer wanted or needed.

Nick, he thought. *Fucking Nick Testa strikes again.*

He put down his knife and fork and started to laugh.

Max was still chuckling back at his desk, when the phone rang. He waited for Next New Girl to pick it up, forgetting for the moment that she had weekends off and was probably on her way home to her budget-class studio apartment in deepest Queens. On the sixth or seventh ring, he picked up the receiver.

"Yo," he said. "Christian Enquiries."

"Oh, for Christ's sake, partner," Tina's voice said, "it's me. I know you're not much of a techie, but don't you at least have caller ID?"

"T, girl," he said, "I was just reading in the papers about how you're a crack homicide detective now. Welcome to the ranks of NYPD legends. That and a MetroCard'll get you a ride on the subway."

"About fucking time I got some shine on me, Sundance. All those years I spent in your shade, and you never even told me once I was the wind beneath your wings. Let alone that it was usually me actually put the case down."

Max laughed. "Sorry about that, girl. Really," he said. "But I was also reading about the killer fridge and your theory that Joey Lips's crew planted the C-4. If I was still on the job, I probably would have guessed ISIS, given the shit they've been pulling. I mean, I never heard of a mob hit with C-4. Have you?"

"Not that I can remember, no."

"But you're buying it this time," Max said. "That really must have been some—what did you call it?—solid intel you had, Joey being on the Beak's hit list and all. I was just curious where it came from."

"Yeah, well, our friend asked me to call you to see if you and I could have dinner with him and Dani tonight up at Bistango. Kind of a family thing. Ali said she'd hook us up with a table, but our friend was worried you'd be pissed at him."

"Pissed at him? For what?"

"Not on the phone, Dance. I thought I'd swing by your shop at like seven, and we can talk about it on the way up there. That's if you're okay with dinner."

"Fuck yeah, T. I'm okay with dinner, and I'm more than okay with our friend. See you then."

"So how you doing, T?" Max said, struggling to keep pace with Tina's hurry-hurry stride; she was a woman of constant purpose, and she saw no purpose in a leisurely stroll, even when she was off duty.

"Doing good," she said. "You heard Briscoe made chief of detectives?"

"Yeah, I saw that on the Squad Room website. One of the few bosses ever to make it without kissing ass all the way up the ladder."

"I know, right?" Tina said. "But wait for it—he took me out to lunch a day or two later and said he wanted to groom me for deputy chief maybe two or three years down the road."

They'd stopped at a red light at Twenty-Fifth Street; the last of the late spring afternoon was balmy, and there were only four blocks to go, but Max was winded and sweating lightly from the forced march up Third Avenue.

"That's great, T," he said. "So what'd you tell him?"

"Long as you've known me, what do you think I told him? I told him no fuckin' way. I told him I live and breathe street, and I'm not about to trade that for an office at One Police Plaza. I told him he could ask me again when I'm maybe sixty."

Max laughed again. They slapped fives and started across the street.

"Besides," Tina said, "the bosses all wear those white shirts, and I look shitty in white. Johnny Cash was the Man in Black; I'm the Woman in Black. Last time I wore anything white was a corsage when Cloudy and I got married, and if they made black carnations, I'da worn them instead."

"I can see why he'd want you. I've been hearing morale in the Bureau has tanked, with all those bureaucratic number bums worried more about stats and overtime than they are about closing cases."

"You heard right, Dance. You thought it was bad in your day? It's worse now, if you can believe that. We've got good police leaving before they've put in their twenty. What's the point in working all night wrapping a case if your boss doesn't even say, 'Nice work. Thank you'? If all he says is no OT?"

"The deputy money'd be nice, though, T," Max said.

"You couldn't pay me enough to move to One PP. I'll never be rich like you, but between Cloudy's practice and my hundred K, we're doing just fine."

They had almost reached Bistango, when she squeezed his arm and said, "So you're pissed at me about the 'solid intel' quote, right? Pissed at Nick too probably."

"Pissed?" Max came to a dead stop at the restaurant door. "How'm I gonna be pissed at either one of you? If it wasn't for your uncle Nick figuring out a strategy and you risking your career to keep the whole thing on the down-low, I wouldn't have my son back. And I'm supposed to be pissed? In fact, I've got a little thank-you gift for you."

He handed Tina a black Tiffany ring box he'd bought on Etsy. She opened it, examined its contents, and looked up at him.

"What's this?" she said.

"It's a flash drive," he said.

"I know it's a fucking flash drive," she said. "What's on it?"

"Everything you ever needed or wanted to know about the Paolucci crime family, set down by its former consigliere and newly anointed don."

"Luca? Jesus, Dance."

"Before you go gaga, you'll never be able to use it as evidence. First of all, it's not the original; it's a copy. Plus, you don't want to know how I happen to have it. But it'll help you put down some open mob murders, and it'll make a great road map for your pal at the Bureau if he wants to start building a RICO case against young Luca and his crew."

Tina pocketed the box, stood on tiptoes, and kissed Max on the lips, a first in their long, asexual friendship. He held the door for her, and they stepped inside.

─ ❖❖❖ ─

Nick arrived everywhere early, being averse to surprises, so Max wasn't surprised to find him and Dani already ensconced at a corner four-top just inside the front window. Neither was their strategic positioning an accident; Nick was, by nature and training, a wary man, and the table gave him clear sight lines to the street, the entrance, and the room, which he scanned at intervals for what he called "potentials"—fellow diners and drinkers who might be trouble.

"Nice vantage point, bro," Max said, slipping into the seat opposite Nick.

"Yeah," Nick said. "The bartender—Ali, right?—saved it for us."

"I'd like to say I briefed her," Tina said, "but all I had to tell her was you're a PI, and she got it. She's known me and Max long enough she doesn't need corner tables with a view explained to her. Ali's one smart lady. Funny too."

"I always liked corners, even when I was a kid," Nick said. "In my DNA, I guess—you know my family tree. I had an uncle, a made man, used to tell me, 'Nico, always remember: what you don't know *can* hurt you.' I know Tina here has the same habits, and I'm guessing you do too after all your years as a cop."

"Had to," Max said. "Made my long-suffering wife nuts when we went out to dinner—me scanning the house every couple minutes like there might be an ax murderer two or three tables away. I tried to break the habit for her sake when I retired, but I couldn't. Still can't."

"You don't mind sitting where you are now, facing a wall?"

"Won't be the first time you had my back, bro."

Nick was reaching for an open bottle of Montepulciano, when Ali appeared tableside, snatched it up, poured him a healthy dose, and topped off Dani's barely touched glass with a splash. "What about you two?" she asked. "Tina, Diet Coke?"

"Naw," Tina said, "I'm off duty, and this is kind of a family

185

reunion, I guess you could call it. Let me have one of those sweet-ass drinks you keep inventing."

"A cranberry margarita sound tempting?"

"Sounds right—long as you don't tell me what all's in it. Way I drink, I'll get hammered just hearing the ingredients."

"Cool," Ali said. "Max, I know you're a creature of habit, but let me pour you a top-shelf bourbon for a change. Woodford Reserve, okay?"

Max was a man of midshelf tastes, but he smiled, nodded, and watched Ali hustle back to her post behind the bar before she was reported AWOL. As if it would have mattered, he thought. Ali had a following. She was a draw, a star.

The boss's comely daughter, Julie, delivered the drinks, and Max lifted a glass to Nick. "*L'chaim*," he said. "A toast of my people. It means 'To life.' I feel I owe mine and my son's to you."

"So we're still friends?" Nick asked.

"Course we're still friends," Max said. "Why wouldn't we be?"

"You saw the papers this morning?"

"Yeah. Sounds like Charlie Beak's fridge got mad at him— all those midnight raids. Your niece here thinks it was Joey Lips did him. I don't guess you'd know anything about it, right?"

Nick stared at Max for a moment, pondering the question. Instead of answering, he asked if anyone at the table had a pen and paper. Tina produced a ballpoint from her jacket and a page from the police-issue memo pad she kept in her hip pocket whether on duty or off. Nick laid the paper on the table, scribbled a message, folded it in two, and passed it to Max. It read,

Don't write anything you can phone. Don't phone anything you can say face-to-face. Don't say anything you can whisper. Don't whisper anything you can smile. Don't smile anything you can nod. Don't nod anything you can wink.

Max looked across the table at Nick. "So you know anything?" he asked.

Nick winked.

Max winked back and laughed loudly enough to draw looks of reproof from the nearby tables. He shoved the note toward Dani. "Want a peek, kid?" he said.

Dani glanced at the paper and then handed it back. "Don't need to," she said. "Testa's laws of human interaction. I grew up with 'em. Know 'em by heart."

"Me too," Tina said, "and they've served me well, Dance. You should keep 'em for future reference."

Max folded the paper into his blazer pocket. He took a deep swallow of bourbon and barely managed to get it down before he started laughing again.

"Easy there, Max," Nick said. "You choke on your drink, you're not getting mouth-to-mouth from me. I'm guessing not these lovely ladies either."

Nick winked. Tina and Dani laughed. Max, with a mighty effort, managed at least the caricature of a poker face.

"So how's the kid doing?" Nick asked.

"Actually, not great so far," Max said. "He's got a lot of catching up to do on his schoolwork, but my wife negotiated a deal with the dean to postpone his finals for as long as he needs. So that part's good. Plus, his coach assigned an assistant to work him out all summer and get him back into game shape for next season."

"Sounds pretty good so far," Tina said. "What's not so great?"

"His girlfriend dumped him. They had a real thing going on, but she doesn't hear from him for two weeks, and, well, you know how women are."

Tina and Dani exchanged looks. "No, Max," Tina said. "Tell us how women are."

"You forget how Cloudy reacted when you had to disappear undercover for, what, five or six days on that case in Chelsea? Moved into some gay-friendly B and B? Whereabouts unknown to anyone?"

"It was twelve days, Dance, and she got over it forthwith."

"Yeah, T, if a month counts as forthwith, and even then, you had to borrow some bucks from me to buy her a ring at Zales—remember that? Women put up with a lot of dumb shit from us guys, but they don't easily forgive and forget a disappearing act. They assume we're off boning someone else."

"Course, you wouldn't know anything about that," Tina said. "Right, Max?"

"Irrelevant and immaterial," Max said. "What matters is Jay's girl won't take his calls or answer his texts, which he didn't need after two weeks in Beak hell. Dew says he's having trouble focusing on his schoolwork—he'll just sit there with a book open in his lap and stare at it for a half hour like he's in some kind of trance. She heard him screaming one night and found him sitting in his boxers on the bedroom floor, brushing his arm over and over like those bullet ants were still there."

"Tell me about it," Nick said. "The kid's got PTSD, and trust me—I know what that's like. I've had it myself since Iraq, and it's no joke."

"Dew wants him to see a shrink," Max said. "You think that'd help?"

"Can't hurt, I guess," Nick said. "But a shrink can't say some magic words or prescribe some magic pills and make PTSD go away, if that's what you're asking. Time helps some— you learn to recognize it and keep it at bay best you can. Try to keep things normal. Stay away from situations that might bring it on."

"Not exactly what you've been doing the last couple weeks," Max said.

"Oh, I'll pay some dues—no doubt about that," Nick said. "I'm okay tonight, but you won't want to be around me the next few days." He smiled. "You won't have to be. Dani and I are headed home first flight out tomorrow," he said. "If I go batshit on the plane, she'll help the crew tranquilize me."

"He's kidding; he doesn't go that kind of batshit," Dani said. "What he does is get the shakes and sweat a lot—that's pretty much it."

"That's pretty much it as far as what you can see," Nick said. "You can't see the flashbacks—the blood, the body parts, your brother dying in your arms. I can. It's like I'm back there, and it's happening all over again."

Max circled the rim of his glass with an index finger for a silent moment. "If that's the cost of war," he said finally, "you've been tempting fate in your time here. I probably would have chosen a different line of work. A desk job. Something peaceful."

"I am who I am; I do what I do," Nick said.

"You're a closer?"

"I'm a closer, and if there's a price attached to that, I'll pay it. It's what I know how to do."

"Maybe this'll help," Max said. He fished a thick brown envelope out of his inside pocket and handed it to Nick across the table.

Nick hefted it. "We agreed on a fee," he said. "This feels too fat."

"Don't worry about it," Max said. "Mission accomplished."

"Thanks, my friend," Nick said.

"No, thank you," Max said. "It was you who did the heavy lifting, and it was you who saved my ass in the woods when Il Lupo was about to take me out."

"But it was you who took him out—you and Ahab. But why don't we adjourn the mutual admiration society meeting and order some chow? We've been here, what, half an hour? We're on our second round of drinks, and we haven't even looked at the menus. Let's fucking eat."

"Yeah, let's," Max said. "But let me ask you one more work question been bugging me. Tina, you're not hearing any of this, okay?"

"My ears are sealed," Tina said.

"Remember when we were putting Luca in the van," Max said, "and you flashed a card at some nosy bystander who tried to get in our way? Backed him off posthaste?"

"Yeah, I remember," Nick said.

"So what was the card?"

"Culinary Institute of America."

"What, where you learn the art of cooking?"

"No, I do some contract jobs for a different outfit with the same initials. Only art of cooking they teach there is how to open an MRE pouch—MREs are meals ready to eat, for you civilians—and see if there's anything inside you're ready to eat. If you got lucky, you'd find some peanut butter and crackers."

"Yummy," Dani said.

"So now can we order?" Nick said. "I'm fucking starved."

"Me too," Max said, "but let's observe a moment of silence for Charlie Beak and pray that the house fridge here isn't mad at us too."

OVERTIME

Max Christian neither accepted nor denied the existence of God, regarding it as a question wholly beyond human understanding. His religion instead was basketball. Its holy city was Harlem, and its mother church was the south court in St. Nicholas Park, where he'd been blooded, bloodied, and finally accepted as a straight-up street baller. That asphalt rectangle had always seemed to him a healing place as well, a world where the pain of a miss lasted only until his next make, and nothing happening in the world beyond its 4,700 square feet seemed to matter.

When Meridew brought Jay home for a late August weekend, Max knew instinctively that an afternoon at Saint Nick South was the next station on his son's journey through rehab. That pilgrimage had been going reasonably well, or so Dew had reported. Jay was getting through his finals with decent grades. His girlfriend, Judith, had forgiven him his weeks of silence once he'd gotten a chance to tell her where he had been. He'd been assured by Coach that once he caught up with his academics, he'd be in the rotation and maybe a starter in the coming season. His night sweats were occasional, and he hadn't wakened screaming in three weeks. He'd been seeing a therapist without protest once a week; the shrink had told Dew ex parte that PTSD was typically a life sentence, but all things considered, Jay was making good progress toward containing it.

Good was nice, kind of like a B-, but Max decided an afternoon of street ball could bump *good* up to *very good*, at least for a day; he knew it had always helped him when he was afflicted by a sore conscience and a lonely heart.

"So'd you bring your gear?" he asked Jay over a late breakfast that Saturday morning. "I was thinking we might go uptown and see if we can get a run. I mean, if you're up for it."

"You kidding, Dad?" Jay said. "I'm not a fucking invalid. Let's do it."

"Fuck yeah," Max said.

"Language, boys," Dew said, but they were already up and moving, en route to their rooms to change into game gear. Within the hour, they were in their sweats and on the A train to Central Harlem.

"Maxi-Pad and L'il' Max!" Black Satin whooped when they walked onto his court. "Couple tourists comin' to the 'hood to study the folkways of the merry Negroes at their play."

"We came for a run," Jay said. "That's if you're not scared to play us. And my name's Jay, not L'il' Max."

"Watch ya mouf, son," Satin said. "You in my house, and I'm the one gives out names up in here. Max, you ain't taught this young'un no better manners than that? Don't know he a minority this part of town?"

Max smiled a mock-sincere smile. "Please accept my most humble apologies on his behalf, kind sir," he said.

"Jus' fuckin' wid you boys," Satin said, flashing a wide smile. "Le's get a game on—half-court, two on two."

"Sounds good," Max said. "White against black?"

"Naw, B, we livin' that every day around here. I'm thinkin' men against boys. Me and you against L'il' Max here and a boy from my academy. Call himself Stacks. He ain't but fifteen, but he got promise." He blew the whistle he kept dangling from a lanyard around his neck. "Yo, Stacks!" he called out. "Here."

The kid called Stacks was sitting on the asphalt with his back against the fence, watching a half-court three-on-three game in vigorous progress. "Coach, me an' my boys got next over here!" he shouted back. "This game almost done."

"You hear me, boy? Get over here 'fore I whip the black off your ass."

Stacks trudged over, his head hanging in submission. His

build was bony, his stance was a slouch, and his walk was bowlegged and slow; by Max's guess, the kid couldn't have been more than five eight or nine. He looked like anything but a baller, but if Satin said he could play, he was a player.

"Okay," Satin said when Stacks finally made it, "it's me and Max here against you an' Li'l' Max. First team to eleven win the game; two games outa three win the day. Le's go."

It took the boys about twenty minutes to dispatch the men two games to none, leaving the losers gasping for breath. Stacks looked bored; he grabbed Jay by the wrist, led him back toward the real action, and hollered, "Next!" Max and Satin sat in place on the tarmac, sweating from the exertion and the muggy dog-day afternoon heat.

"Li'l' Max did okay out there, poppin' them midrange jumpers," Satin said. "He can play."

"Yeah, Jay's got a nice J—better'n his old man's," Max said. "He could up his game if he learns to take it to the hole more and mix it up a little. He's still learning."

"Learnin' good it look like," Satin said.

"Yeah," Max said, "but you and I both know it was the kid Stacks owned the court. You weren't joking when you said he's got game. Little guy was doing it all out there—he can run, he can pass, he can dunk, he can shoot the three, he can play D, he sees the court like a pro."

It took Satin a moment to answer. "I'm prayin' for the shorty, cuz," he said, "an' I ain't what you'd call a church-goin' man."

"Praying for him?" Max asked. "Why? It's anyone playing against him needs to pray."

"Prayin' 'cause I'm fighting the street for his soul. I know what it is 'cause I been in these streets, and they don't lead nowhere but a dead end."

"Literally dead sometimes," Max said.

"Yeah, like in-the-ground dead. The boy was s'posed to be in middle school, but he was spending his days here ballin' and his nights on the corners, doin' who know what. Got to a point his auntie he live with calls me. Says she heard about the 'cademy. That's how she said it—'cademy. And could I take him in an' set him on the path of righteousness? That's the way she put it."

"So you did it?"

"Took him in, yeah. Still workin' on the path. I had a couple my seniors tutor him. Helped get his GPA up to where we could let him play, an' you seen what he can do. Two or three Division I scouts been by our games to check him out. One of 'em told me another year, the boy got McDonald's High School All-American potential."

"Sounds like he's maybe found that path," Max said. "So what's the problem?"

"Problem is, I don't know what he doin' after dark," Satin said. "His auntie don't either, 'cept he ain't home hittin' the books. I can't be with him twenty-four-seven."

"Oh boy."

"Yeah," Satin said. "So how L'il' Max doin', cuz? I mean, other than tunin' up his game. I know he been through a lot up there in Beak House."

Max smiled. "You read some Dickens in the joint?" he asked.

"Yeah, *Bleak House* was part of my white studies syllabus. You read enough Dickens, you see y'all ofay ancestors come from way more primitive tribes than ours did. For real. Half the South settled by small-time cutpurses weren't bad enough to hang, and *they* owned *us*? Honky, please."

"I'm gonna let that pass for now," Max said. "You asked about Jay, and pretty much all I can tell you is he's doing better. He's just not whole yet. I'll tell you, though—today's doing him a lot of good. Hell of a lot."

"Anytime he in town, B, he welcome on my court, whether you with him or not. Up here, you got game, you can play, and L'il' Max showed me some today. For a young'un, he got game. Like his daddy used to."

"You mean for a white young'un, right?" Max said. "I mean, you being a racist and all?"

"No, I mean young. You an' me gettin' old—'specially you. I heard you been workin' out on that short court down by Fourth Street, tryin' to dunk and can't get above the rim no more. Players down there talkin' 'bout Mighty Whitey a step short of checkin' into the ol'-folk home."

They were trading fives and laughing, when a scuffle under the far backboard escalated to a full-blown melee. Satin lifted himself to his feet and strode to midcourt. His whistle shrieked. Everyone froze.

"Stop!" he bellowed. "I don't book this kinda shit in my house. All y'all get off the court right now—you done for the day, and if any of y'all come back tomorrow, I don't wanna hear no 'Next!' All y'all be last in line."

Someone among the miscreants said something Max couldn't hear.

"Don't make no never mind to me who started what—all y'all need to get gone. Who got next? Stacks? It's your court."

Stacks led his crew onto the battlefield, and Max felt a surge of relief mixed with pride at seeing Jay among them; there could be nothing as restorative as being chosen as a teammate by the best player on the court. He struggled upright and found a seat on a bench nearer the action just in time to see Jay take a slick no-look pass from Stacks and pop a fifteen-footer.

He was about to cheer the shot, when the long-gone shade of Camus took form out of a multicolored eddy of dust motes beside him. Max fumbled for the BlackBerry in the hip pocket of his cutoffs and pressed it to his ear so he wouldn't look like a crazy old white man talking to himself.

"Ya boy know what to do wid that rock it look like," Camus said. "He comin' along good otherwise?"

"Let's just say he's coming along," Max said. "*Good* would be overstating it right now. *Better* would be better."

"You got it right bringin' him here. Peoples think ballin' just a game, but pretty near e'rything I know about right an' wrong come from my days playin' football. Talkin' 'bout what y'all call soccer, case you ain't heard."

"I figured that's why you finally came back—to give me another lecture about right and wrong."

"Don't be callin' it no lecture, son. Jus' some wisdom from

a old dude been around more'n a hunnit years, countin' my time livin' an' dead."

"Well, let me give *you* a bit of wisdom, Al. Don't be wearing that wool overcoat on a muggy August day in New York. The feels-like temperature is ninety-four."

"You see me sweatin', boy? I'm a ghos'—you forgot? A ghos' don't feel no weather. We steady cool at all times."

"Okay, okay, so let's get on with it," Max said. "You're upset with me over how I got my son back, right?"

"You an' the boy Nick you runnin' with. The two of you carryin' a lot of bodies behind this whole mess."

"Am I proud of the body count? No, I'm not. But Nick was my friend in need, and we did what had to be done to get my son home alive."

"Yeah, well, you say you ain't proud, but I was knockin' down Courvoisiers wid my boo Edie Wharton up in Ghost Town, and we seen you on TV laughin' at what y'all friend in need done to this man Charlie Beak—I get his name right?"

"You got it right, and he deserved what he got. The guy was a monster. He kept my son alive the whole time so he could torture us all—Jay physically and me and my wife mentally. When you saw me laughing, I was laughing at myself, really, 'cause Nick did what I should've done but couldn't."

"You couldn't 'cause ya conscience told you no?"

"I just couldn't. I don't know—I guess the brothers up this way would say I ain't built like that. Nick is, and I'm okay with what he did."

"You okay this Beak got blowed up in his own kitchen? Wha'd the paper say—nothin' left but sliced deli meat?"

"I'm okay with the bottom line, which is there's one less merchant of death out here poisoning these streets with drugs. Nick does things his way; I do things mine. If you're a cop like I was, you get used to waiting out the processes of the law. If you were special ops in Iraq like Nick was, you don't wait—hesitation can get you killed. The two of us travel different roads, but we share the same goal—justice."

"You sayin' the end justify the means," Camus said. "Like I tol' you the other day, they's some means can't no way be excused, and I believe that yet today. And don't be remindin' me I was okay with hangin' my countrymen who got caught collaboratin' with the Nazis durin' the war. I had my regrets since, but in a war, they ain't no time for moralizin'. You heard?"

"Exactly what I'm saying, Al," Max said. "We were in a war, we won it, and not just my family but my city are better off for it. Another thing you wrote back in the day—if we can't reduce the sum of evil in the world, we can at least not add to it. Well, guess what, my old friend? We didn't add to it—we fucking reduced it, and we brought my boy home in the process."

"By any means necessary? Like you yaself said?"

"I'll live with the means, and if you're asking me to throw Nick under the bus, I won't. I like the guy. I hope we get to work together again. And if we do or don't, we at least rid the world of a guy who calls himself, accurately, a student of pain. By which he meant other people's pain, not his."

Camus smiled. "We all students of pain, son," he said. "I study reducin' it. Ya boy Nick study causin' it. An' you? You like most peoples—the pain you mostly studyin' is your own."

"You think?" Max asked, knowing it was true.

"I think," Camus said, starting to evanesce. "But I gots to bounce now. New York always scheduled tight for me. Later, B."

Max glanced up court just as Stacks flipped a high-lob pass to Jay, who caught it one-handed above the rim and jammed it home for the deciding basket. The winners were whooping, high-fiving, low-fiving, chest-bumping, and calling for the threesome who had next to get their asses onto the asphalt.

Jay cut loose from the pack and jogged over to Max's end of the bench, pebbled with sweat and flushed with victory. "Dad, you see that?" he said. "How high I got on that dunk?"

Max embraced him. "Yeah, I saw it, Son," he said. "That was great. Made your old man jealous—you up there talking to God like that."

"You mind if we stay awhile, Dad?" Jay said. "There's another game in a minute, and Stacks wants me back."

Max looked at his son with new eyes. He saw the Jay he'd thought he lost. His smile was bright, his eyes were alive, and his stance was unbowed. He was the boy waiting for a yes from his dad, who in fact was fighting to keep back tears.

"We'll stay long as you want, Jaybird," Max said. "Welcome home."

AN AFTERWORD FROM THE AUTHOR

The first rule of my past life as a journalist was "Don't make stuff up." When you cross over into crime fiction, as I have, that changes; making stuff up is what you do. You draw on life experience and not just your own; writers, as the late author and filmmaker Nora Ephron put it, are cannibals. You use scraps of what you see and hear (or overhear) on the street. You go to Google for the nomenclature of a SIG Sauer pistol, the pay scale for NYPD detectives, or the locations of the world's most exotic tax havens. But you also learn to rely on friends to fill in blanks in your own knowledge, and I'd like to express my gratitude to some of them here.

I'll start with three warriors who served with valor and honor in America's thankless war in Vietnam. Sergeant Lee Reagan did four tours in-country as a Green Beret. Ed "Hook" Kazarian was an LRRP, a much-decorated member of a long-range reconnaissance patrol team. Kazarian won a chestful of medals in 'Nam but lost a hand in combat—hence his nickname—and ultimately his life; he died long after the war of exposure to the chemical defoliant Agent Orange.

I know these two men only indirectly; their deeds and skills were channeled for me by their brother warrior, the man who appears in these pages as Nicola Malatesta, a.k.a. Nick Testa. We were introduced in 2015 by our close mutual friend Karen Mullarkey, to whom I owe an extraspecial thank-you for her role as matchmaker. Nicola and I come from different worlds. I'm a man of words; he's a man of action. My detective, Max, is imaginary; Nicola is a PI in gritty real life. But the two of us bonded in friendship, and he became a vital contributor to this book, not just as a consultant on the arts of war but also as a principal new member of my ongoing company of players.

So it would not be wholly accurate to say that any resemblance between the characters in this book and any real-world person, living or dead, is coincidental. Apart from Mr. Malatesta, I've used the real first names of real staffers at real New York restaurants and bars. Albert Camus was, of course, a real French novelist, playwright, essayist, journalist, and philosopher. His thoughts, expressed here not in French but in the language of the black American street, reflect his real-world views on life, good, and evil, and I hope I've done them justice in translation. His ghost and his residence in Ghost Town, over near the sky, are wholly products of my own fevered imagination, as are all the earthly characters in this tale.

My further debts proliferate. A lot of friends helped with facts, home truths, advice, and sustenance during those days and weeks when the muse forgot my address and phone number. Among them, besides Ms. Mullarkey, are Sala Andaiye, Susan Fraker, Cindy Kazarian, Rita Reidy Lennick, Paul Darwin Lee, Al Manzello, Betsy Neer, Joan Reidy, Alison Rodda, Verna Mae Seño, Robert Spitzler, and Jessica Watson. I might not be doing this at all if it weren't for the ongoing encouragement I've received from my dear friend Robert Littell, who ranks with the Amblers, Le Carrés, and Graham Greenes as a tale-teller of espionage and political intrigue.

Finally, I owe a special thank-you to my friend and former *Newsweek* colleague Sarah Crichton, now doyenne of her own imprint at Farrar, Straus, and Giroux. She has been the source of wise counsel on my segue from journalist to novelist and on finding a place for the tales of Max Christian on the crowded shelves of crime fiction.

Printed in the United States
By Bookmasters